THE EIGHTH URBAN FARM FRESH ROMANCE

Glimpses of Gossamer

VALERIE COMER

GreenWords Media

ACKNOWLEDGMENTS

Thank you for being a faithful reader of the Urban Farm Fresh Romance series!

Thanks to Elizabeth Maddrey, first reader, idea-bouncer and excellent author in your own right. Thank you for providing sanity, humor, and kicks in the pants as needed!

Also thank you to beta readers Paula and Gretchen. Your comments helped tighten and improve this story! Also thanks to Marcia for naming the heroine, Marley Montgomery. We do have fun in the Facebook Reader Group, don't we!

A big thank you to my fabulous editor, Nicole, who sees beyond words, punctuation, and sentence structure to the heart of the story.

I'm also grateful for the Christian Indie Authors Facebook group and my sister bloggers at Inspy Romance. These folks make a difference in my life every single day. I'm thrilled to walk beside them as we tell stories for Jesus!

Thank you to my Facebook friends, followers, street

team, and reader group members for prayers, encourage-
ment, and great fellowship.

Thanks to my husband, Jim, for research trips to
Spokane and talking through scenarios as needed — to say
nothing of everyday love and support — and to my kids and
grandgirls for cheering me on and embracing the idiosyn-
crasies of having an author for a mom and grandmother.

All my love and gratitude goes to Jesus, the One who
invited me to experience His unending and passionate love
and walks beside me every day. My prayer is that you see
His love anew through the pages of this story.

Valerie Comer Bibliography

Urban Farm Fresh Romance

0. Promise of Peppermint (ebook only)
1. Secrets of Sunbeams
2. Butterflies on Breezes
3. Memories of Mist
4. Wishes on Wildflowers
5. Flavors of Forever
6. Raindrops on Radishes
7. Dancing at Daybreak
8. Glimpses of Gossamer

Saddle Springs Romance
(Montana Ranches Christian Romance)

1. The Cowboy's Christmas Reunion
2. The Cowboy's Mixed-Up Matchmaker
3. The Cowboy's Romantic Dreamer
4. The Cowboy's Convenient Marriage
5. The Cowboy's Belated Discovery
6. The Cowboy's Reluctant Bride

Christmas in Montana Romance

1. More Than a Tiara
2. Other Than a Halo
3. Better Than a Crown

Garden Grown Romance
(Arcadia Valley Romance)

1. Sown in Love (ebook only)
2. Sprouts of Love
3. Rooted in Love
4. Harvest of Love

Farm Fresh Romance

1. Raspberries and Vinegar
2. Wild Mint Tea
3. Sweetened with Honey
4. Dandelions for Dinner
5. Plum Upside Down
6. Berry on Top

Riverbend Romance Novellas

1. Secretly Yours
2. Pinky Promise
3. Sweet Serenade
4. Team Bride
5. Merry Kisses

valeriecomer.com/books

A truck engine cut out in Marley Montgomery's driveway. She peeked out the window and inhaled a sharp breath at the sight of a white truck. Its logo read SCRAPS, with the words Spokane County Regional Animal Protection Service surrounding it. Oh, no. What was animal control doing here? She had a mighty good guess, and there wouldn't be any evidence by the time the officer finished gathering her things, exited the truck, and rang the doorbell.

Marley dodged around unpacked boxes and out the backdoor into the wildflower-infested yard. Chickens. Where were the chickens? She had too many for the city's bylaws, but she hadn't been able to resist the adorable Silkies. She hadn't been able to bear the responsibility of parting any of them from their friends.

At least the hens had friends. Marley didn't. Not anymore. But she'd make new ones here in Bridgeview, if only she didn't run afoul of the laws. She took a swipe at Bianca and tossed her over the nearest fence. She'd figure out how to get her back later, hopefully before the home-owner returned. Chloe followed, then Deirdre. She just needed to find two more. Any two.

The front doorbell chimed, the sound barely audible through the house.

She had mere seconds left. Where was Gloria? The Buff Orpington loved the deep shade in the far corner, close to the chain-link fence. Marley reached into the spot behind the compost bin, felt fluffy feathers, and snagged the bird. She pivoted and let Gloria fly.

"Good afternoon!"

Marley wiped her hands down her flouncy skirt and eyed the uninvited — and unwanted — visitor who stepped into view beyond the chain-link fence at the opposite corner of the house. Hopefully the woman hadn't seen that little maneuver.

She was roughly Marley's age with red-gold hair in a long braid over one shoulder. A duty belt emphasized her uniform with its spray can and a radio. If she wore a gun, it wasn't visible.

"Hi." Marley approached the gate, pushing her guilty conscience aside and managing a smile.

"Hi. I'm Eden Riehl, and I work for Spokane County Regional Animal Protection Service." The woman touched the logo on her dark blue shirt. "I'm here to investigate a grievance that this property is housing more poultry than zoning allows."

"I'm sorry to hear there's been a complaint." Marley kept the smile in place. Which neighbor? The old man on the east, or the houseful of apparently single men on the west? She needed to start offering free eggs to both sides now that the hens had settled in and were laying again.

Only now it would look like bribery.

The officer angled her head and raised her eyebrows. "Are you?"

Marley blinked. "Am I what?"

Ms. Riehl sighed, pulled out a digital pad, and tapped the screen, which she scanned. "This city lot is thirty feet wide at the front, wider at the back, and one hundred feet deep, a roughly pie shape which comes to five thousand square feet. Regulations stipulate you may house up to five chickens *or* two small livestock *or* one small livestock and two chickens." She tapped her stylus and eyed Marley. "How many chickens live on this property?"

"Um…" Marley's mind raced. Honesty might be the best policy, generally speaking, but what was she supposed to do with her extras? Her stepdad would have laughed and said, 'soup pot,' but a girl didn't eat her friends. "I thought the property was bigger." She waved up the steep, irregular hillside behind the house. "The pegs are way up there somewhere. Surely it's more than you said."

"What size did you think?" The officer's shaped eyebrows angled upward.

Marley wasn't admitting anything. "I, um, thought it was quite a lot bigger."

"Ms… I'm sorry. I don't believe I got your name."

"Marley Montgomery."

"Ms. Montgomery, it's your duty to learn the local laws for animal husbandry, the specific regulations for your particular lot and neighborhood, and then follow them."

Hard to argue with that. She nodded cautiously.

"Are you the homeowner here or a renter?"

"In transition." Marley swallowed hard, tears welling in her eyes. "Gram Renton is still the owner, but she's in a nursing home now with advanced Alzheimer's. I'm her heir." Still hard to believe.

The officer's stance softened. "I'm sorry to hear that. Do the chickens in question belong to Mrs. Renton?"

Marley stared at her bare toe poking at the too-long grass. "No."

"I hope you understand I need to investigate the complaint. May I enter the yard?"

Zephyr was often hidden in a back corner, and only two or three were likely to rush to Marley's side. After her little cleanup operation, she was only one bird over. It would probably be okay. She nodded and shifted away from the gate.

Ms. Riehl stepped through it and looked around. "Wow, you've got a lot going on here."

"No one has cared for the yard in several years, so it's a bit overgrown." A bit. Now *that* was an understatement, but Marley loved the crazy wildness of it. She and Gram Renton would have gotten along great if they'd ever had the opportunity.

"I see that. I never met the previous owner." Ms. Riehl moved down the overgrown path, peering under bushes.

That was an odd comment. Spokane was a city of several hundred thousand people. Most residents never met. Unless the animal control officer meant no one had ever complained about the owner before. Figured Marley'd be the one to get this address registered in the complaint book.

"Oh, she's sweet." Ms. Riehl bent and patted Bella. "I have a Silkie who looks a lot like her. And she loves attention just as much."

Huh. What was the appropriate response? Marley couldn't think of one.

The officer glanced over at her, but then her gaze went beyond, turning quizzical. She straightened, all her attention now focused on the yard next door.

Marley pinned her smile in place.

"Since when do Alex and Peter have chickens?" The woman muttered as she strode over to the fence, hands on her hips.

Uh oh. Marley swallowed hard. *Be sure your sins will find you out.* Reverend Smith had preached on that a bunch of times, and the truth may have just caught up with her.

The officer plucked a black feather off the top of the chain-link fence and turned to Marley, eyebrows raised. "Would you happen to know anything about this?"

In the yard next door, Deirdre fluffed her feathers with gusto in a raised garden bed amid tidy rows of bush beans. Marley held in her gasp. She needed to get her hens back in her own yard before they did any irreparable damage. It was always best to be on good terms with the neighbors.

"Ms. Montgomery?" The woman's voice turned chilly.

"I, um..."

"Are those your birds?"

Marley squeezed her eyes shut then met the officer's gaze. She was so, so sunk. "Maybe? Yes?"

Ms. Riehl's lips tightened. "I suggest you catch them and return them home, and then we'll discuss your infraction."

Not good. Why, oh why had she thought the city bylaws were more like suggestions? Thought no one would care if she was a couple of birds over? Okay, possibly more than a couple, but they were sweethearts, and they'd been raised as chicks together. She hadn't had the heart to separate them. Didn't girls need each other?

Not that Marley knew for sure, since she'd been on her own most of her life. But *if* she'd had the chance to be part of a flock like her hens, she'd have been devastated to be separated from them.

Marley caught sight of Ms. Riehl striding for the gate. Better follow. Better obey. She wasn't cut out to be a rebel. Not really.

⌒‿ℓ‿ℓ

ALEX SANTORO PEDALED his commuter bicycle up the steep incline into his carport and swung off. He removed his briefcase from the rear rack before lifting the bike to its hooks under the rafters. Then he picked up the briefcase and headed for the back steps, unclipping his bike helmet as he went.

The squawk of a chicken and a flurry of activity assailed him. What on earth? Eden Riehl grabbed for the legs of a mostly white bird, who flapped her wings and sidled away. The new next-door neighbor, whom Alex had seen a few times in her backyard, picked up another one and tossed it over the tall fence. There were at least two other chickens loose in his yard.

Was there a hole somewhere? But then why was Eden here, in uniform? He'd seen her work truck parked in the drive next door but hadn't thought anything of it.

The garden bed nearest the fence was a shamble with uprooted plants and mounds of black earth where it had been flat, smooth, and weed-free this morning. A model garden.

No more.

Alex set his gear on the bottom step. "What's going on here?" he demanded.

Eden and the other woman straightened, pivoting toward him.

Alex skewered the new neighbor with his gaze then slowly raised his eyebrows.

"Hi?" She swept her long reddish-blond tangles away from her eyes, revealing a pretty face, younger than he'd assumed.

But wide-eyed innocence wasn't going to cut it. Not when her poultry created havoc in the gardens he and his family depended on for their business, Bridgeview Backyards. Well, mostly his cousin Peter, since Alex had kept his day job in an air-conditioned office, while their other partner, Alex's sister, Jasmine, had recently given birth to her first baby. The fledgling business had hired a couple of teenage boys to help Peter through the coming busy summer.

The woman still stared at him while the hen that had escaped Eden flapped toward the house.

Alex shook his head and reached for the bird. He caught the legs easily, dangling it upside down from his hand. "Eden? What do you want me to do with this?"

Eden speared a nasty look at the still-unnamed woman. "I'll take her to one of the truck kennels." She snatched the bird out of his hand and headed to the carport.

"No, please!" The other woman's gaze toggled between Alex and Eden. "You can't take Bianca. She's been with her sisters all her life."

Bianca?

Eden's lips tightened as she shook her head slightly and continued on her way.

The other woman ran after her, tears flowing down her cheeks.

Alex stepped in front of her. "Who are you, and what is going on here?" She tried to dodge past him, but he shifted sideways. "You're on my property. I think the least you can do is explain."

She turned imploring eyes toward him. "But... Bianca!"

"Who *are* you?"

She gathered her long curls over her shoulder then her gaze ricocheted off his. "Marley. Marley Montgomery." She thumbed to the ramshackle house on the east side of Alex's. "I moved in there a few days ago."

"Are you related to Gram Renton?"

Her eyes dropped, and her bare toe scuffed in his freshly mown grass. "Sort of?"

"How can you be sort of related to someone?"

She bit her lip, and a pretty pink lip it was.

Alex gave his head a quick shake. He was not here to admire a woman's lips, especially not this woman's. Not someone who did not respect fences and boundaries but interfered with his well-ordered life.

Marley peeked up. "She was my biological father's foster mom for a couple of years."

He jolted back, slamming his calf against the wooden step. Wow, those words had been packed with a lot of anguish. Drama he knew little about, thank the Lord, coming from a large, close-knit family. He was fourth of five siblings and had been raised in a solid Christian home with his Italian nonna and most of his uncles, aunts, and cousins living within a few blocks. He'd had it good. He knew that.

But it wasn't reason enough to let his neighbor run roughshod over him or make a play for his sympathy. "Get your chickens out of here and patch the hole in the fence." Had that been too rude? "Please," he added.

Her spine straightened and her eyes skewered his. "There's no hole."

Alex raised his eyebrows. "So how did they get into my yard, then? They're your birds, and it's your duty to keep them contained."

From beside him, Eden spoke in a wry tone. "And it's my duty to make sure the property is left with no more than five birds. So, if you'll round up that last one, please, I'll put her in the kennel, and we'll go count what's remaining next door."

Marley's eyes filled with tears. "But you can't."

"Honey." Eden's voice sounded like Marley had gotten on her last nerve. "City regulations are clear. You have too many chickens, and I'm removing some of them. It's my job."

"What will happen to them?" Marley's lips quivered.

Lips again. Alex jerked his gaze away. Either his new neighbor was the ultimate drama queen, or she truly felt deeply for those stupid birds. Could she really be this good an actor?

"Hopefully we can find a good home for them." Eden sighed. "Would you please grab that hen?"

"You said you had chickens of your own. Surely you understand." Marley's gaze brightened. "Maybe you could take them yourself."

"My lot is the same size as yours, and I'm maxed out with a goat and two hens."

Those blue eyes widened. "You have a goat?" she asked in breathless wonder.

She couldn't possibly be performing. "Eden's goat's name is Pansy," offered Alex. "Good milk."

"You know each other." It wasn't a question.

"Bridgeview is a tight neighborhood. Everyone knows everyone." And Alex liked it that way. It was uncomfortable for people who had things to hide, though Alex's brother Basil had managed to mask a drinking problem before running a police roadblock nearly two years back and getting slapped with a DUI.

"Please help me find a home for them," Marley pleaded. She turned to Alex. "Maybe you? I can take care of them here. You don't need to worry about a thing."

His jaw dropped. "Me? Have you seen the mess they made? We're running an organic food box program here."

She swallowed hard and looked down. "I understand."

Everything she thought flew across her face. He hated being manipulated, but, man! How could he say no to her? Yet, he had to stand firm. His business depended on it.

2

*M*arley could barely see through her tears as she picked up Chloe and cuddled the Silkie to her chest. Chloe, sweetheart that she was, leaned into it. If chickens could purr, this one would totally be rumbling.

If only Marley had handled this differently, but she hadn't. The animal control officer was waiting to cage Chloe along with Gloria, Bianca, and Deirdre. Then, no doubt, Ms. Riehl would do a thorough search of Marley's yard and find the six remaining birds. Would she remove all of them because Marley had broken the law? Could Marley barter which ones to keep? But how could she part with any of them?

Be a grownup, Marley.

Some days, she hated adulting, though it was an improvement over wondering when someone would get in her face for insubordination. A more terrible thought attacked her. They wouldn't send her to jail, would they? Surely this wasn't that big a crime. But how could she be sure? She should've thought things through before accepting that little flock of Silkies.

"Ms. Montgomery?" The woman's voice sounded devoid of patience.

"I'll put her in the kennel myself." Would she be able to resist letting them all out of the truck? She had to thwart the thought. She couldn't do her friends any good if she were arrested.

"How many more birds are in your yard?" The officer's foot tapped. "Not that I can take your word for it after this."

"I understand." Marley swallowed a lump in her throat. "There are six more. I'll find Ginger for you."

"I'll need to do a complete search." The woman pointed to the driveway. "Come along now."

Marley scrubbed her hand across her eyes to clear her vision. The homeowner frowned slightly as he stared at her. Yeah, she was that pathetic. He was cute in a preppy way. Too bad she'd gotten off on the wrong foot. He wore dressy black pants and a pale gray button-down shirt, a black tie loosened at the throat. His dark hair was cropped short, still managing to be a tiny bit unruly. If he let it grow, there might be curls. Clear blue eyes looked straight at her, straight *into* her. What did he see?

"There might be an option."

She blinked at his voice, softened from a few minutes before.

He broke eye contact, turning to the officer. "Didn't Kass and Wesley say something about wanting to get into birds this year? I could give them a call and see if they've made a final decision."

Hope surged in Marley's heart.

Eden gave him a hard glare then shrugged slightly. "Sure. Phone them. You've got a few minutes while I complete the census next door."

The guy pulled a cell phone out of his pocket.

Marley stepped closer, still clutching Chloe. "Thanks. I don't even know your name." Which seemed a crying shame when he was trying to help.

"Alex Santoro."

"Well, thank you, Alex. I'm sorry about all this mess. I promise I'll come over and clean it up as best I can as soon as we're done."

She didn't miss his slightly raised eyebrows as he glanced next door. So he thought she couldn't tidy a yard because she happened to have a wild mass of flowers and herbs in her own? She'd been there less than a week, for crying out loud, and she wasn't going to go around ripping out all those plants without considering the merits of each one.

"I can do it myself, but thanks." His blue eyes had chilled a little.

"I insist." Though she shouldn't. She didn't even know the guy. He might be... weird... though he didn't give off that vibe. And she should know.

His chin lifted as his eyebrows rose.

Marley's temper flared, but she bit back hasty words. Chloe protested the tight hold Marley had around her, but that was just too bad. Wait, now he probably wouldn't help her. She paused before entering the carport and glanced back, but he had his phone to his ear already, his gaze still fixed on her.

"Wesley? Hey, man. How are you guys doing?"

Marley wasn't going to stand there and eavesdrop or

make faces at Alex's end of the conversation. She pivoted toward the street.

Ms. Riehl tapped her foot at the bottom of the driveway. "Can we proceed without further delays?"

"I'm sorry." How could she give up Chloe, though? How could she help this woman capture and remove half her flock? They'd probably end up on someone's dinner plate. Grief clenched her gut, and her hands trembled as she tucked Chloe into the truck kennel with her friends.

With a heavy heart and empty hands, Marley led the way along the side of her house and through the gate. She'd brought this on herself, just as she always did. She needed to squelch her impulsive nature. Hadn't her stepfather tried to smack it out of her repeatedly? A wise woman would have learned by now.

Ms. Riehl set a plastic kennel down beside the gate as several chickens ran out to see what the excitement was. Marley watched as the officer scooped them into the kennel then left to deliver them to the truck.

Only three left. Ginger rushed over, and Marley picked her up. Tears streaming down her face, she passed her over to Ms. Riehl without a word.

Two more. The officer searched the property, found them, and removed them. Then she crisscrossed the space several more times before looking over at Marley sitting on the back step. "Total of ten?" she asked.

"Yes, ma'am." Marley's voice broke.

The other woman sat down beside her. "I know you hate me right now, but please understand my situation here. I was one of the citizens who fought hard for the right to have livestock within city limits a few years back. Enforcing animal bylaws is my job. I'm not gleefully snatching chickens from every yard I can find. Yours are beautiful birds, and I'm sure you've been taking very good care of them."

Marley managed a nod.

"You may come down to the truck and select five hens to return to your yard."

"What happens to the others?" She turned watery eyes to the officer.

Ms. Riehl gazed at her with compassion. "I'll do my best to find a good home for them, but don't count on it until it happens."

That sounded ominous, but Marley was out of options. "Okay."

A deep voice spoke from over by the fence. "Wesley says he'll talk it over with Kass when she gets home from work."

Hope sprang. "Thank you."

Alex held up a hand. "Don't thank me yet. It's far from a done deal. Kass is due to have a baby in a few weeks. It might be a bad time for them."

The officer rested a hand on her own belly for a brief instant.

Marley narrowed her gaze. Was the woman expecting? She did look a little thick there compared to her otherwise slight build.

Marley was never going to have kids. The world was overpopulated as it was, and she knew what it was like to be unwanted. Nope. It was going to be her and her chickens in this gorgeous old cottage until she was locked in a nursing home like Gram Renton. She'd just be thankful this fantastic opportunity had dropped into her lap when she'd been at the end of her rope. No more messing up like with the chickens. From here on out, she'd be a model citizen, keep to herself, and create just enough art to pay her taxes and buy a few groceries.

She wouldn't need to buy eggs. The five remaining birds would keep her in plenty of those.

Five hens. It was up to Marley to decide who lived.

AFTER WAITING for Eden to drive away then changing into a pair of shorts and a T-shirt, Alex knelt beside the raised garden bed and reached for one of the uprooted bean plants. It looked a little worse for wear, but it might survive.

What on earth had his new neighbor been thinking? He shook his head, stifling a chuckle at the tears over a few stupid chickens. Marley. That was her name. She'd moved into Gram Renton's dilapidated cottage about a week ago. He'd seen her a couple of times, long curly hair hiding her face, a baggy top and long skirt hiding her body.

He'd been waiting for Peter and Sadie to have a few minutes when the three of them could go over and introduce themselves. Maybe bring a welcome basket filled with veggies.

A soft sound brought him out of his reverie, and he glanced over to find Marley kneeling across from him wearing battered old gardening gloves. She smoothed the soil and reached for an upended plant.

He glanced at the weed-filled lot visible through the fence. If she knew anything about gardening, why not start over there? He had this part covered. "I told you not to worry about it." Maybe his voice was gruffer than it ought to be.

"I know." She glanced at him and then back to her hands patting black soil around the bean plant. "But it's my fault."

Totally true, and short of physically removing her, he was stuck with her now. "Okay. I'll run the watering system when we're done. A good soaking should help the roots settle back in."

"You must know a lot about growing vegetables."

A puff of pride billowed his chest. "Quite a bit. My parents have had a garden forever, and us kids put in our fair share of weeding and helping with the harvest."

She glanced up at him from behind her veil of hair. "I've never had a garden, but I'd like to try. Is June too late?"

He rocked back on his heels and studied her.

"Unless you think it doesn't really help with the budget. I need to cut costs where I can."

Even more interesting. The thrifty accountant in Alex approved. "You can save quite a lot, depending on how much you grow." He glanced through the fence. "Did Mrs. Renton ever have a garden back there?"

"She's got dementia, so there's little point in asking her. I hoped you'd know."

"I only bought this place a couple of years ago. It's looked like that the whole time." Peter had gone over to see if they could use the yard to grow produce for Bridgeview Backyards, but the old woman had slammed the door in his face. Weed pods continued to blow their sticky, floaty seeds across in every summer breeze. Maybe that would end with Marley's garden. A guy could hope.

Marley shifted to the next plant. "I know it will be a lot of work, but I have time. If it isn't too late in the season."

"It's not too late." But Alex didn't know anyone who had a lot of time. "Where do you work?"

"I, um..." She shot him a quick glance and patted the soil. "I hope to work from home. I'm an artist."

"An artist?" He couldn't keep the incredulity out of his voice. What kind of career path was that? Sure, Wesley Ferguson made a decent living with his sculptures made of found and recycled objects, but he sold to museums and art collectors. He was no beginner hoping to strike gold. Yet the path seemed to suit Marley, scatterbrained and silly as she must be to throw hens over the fence without a care for the adjacent homeowner.

"What's so weird about that?"

He'd keep his thoughts to himself. "Nothing."

They worked in silence for a few minutes then she cleared her throat. "So, about a garden. What do I need to do?"

"Start with digging up the area to get rid of the weeds and their roots."

She frowned at him. "The weeds?"

Alex raised his eyebrows. She couldn't see weeds over there? Was she blind?

"There are a lot of wildflowers and herbs." Marley sighed. "And I'm sure some weeds. I haven't had the chance to look them all up yet to be sure."

Wildflowers and herbs? She'd get on well with Alex's sister. But weren't the thistles and thorns and dandelions self-explanatory?

"To have a garden, you'll need to clear an area or put in a raised bed or two. Then it depends on what veggies you prefer."

She shrugged. "I'm not picky. What's easy to grow?"

"Well, spinach and peas and radishes like the cooler weather of early spring. But you could still plant beans or carrots or..." It really would help to know what she liked. Besides, Peter and Jasmine were the expert gardeners, not Alex. Give him a spreadsheet any day of the week over soil analysis and succession planting. "But you'd need to dig up a patch and test the pH first."

"pH? What's that?"

Gardening 101, he could do. "How much acid is in your soil affects how things will grow. Some plants, like blueberries, like it more acidic. But a lot of veggies prefer a more alkaline base."

"Oh. I guess I'll need to do some research."

"Probably. Google knows everything."

"If you ask the right questions."

"True that." His estimation of her kicked up a notch. Maybe she wasn't as naive as she'd seemed at first.

"Hey, guys! Whoa, what happened here?"

Alex glanced over his shoulder to see Peter and Sadie at the back of the carport, holding hands. "A bit of a mishap. Hopefully everything will recover."

Sadie looked between him and Marley.

Okay, fine, he'd introduce her around. Alex rose and dusted his gardening gloves together. "Peter, Sadie, this is our new next-door neighbor, Marley Montgomery." He thumbed toward the nearby fence, not that they didn't know which house. "Marley, this is my cousin Peter. He lives with me for now. His fiancée, Sadie Guthrie, lives in the big old house on the other side."

Sadie dragged Peter closer. "I'm so pleased to meet you, Marley. We've been meaning to come over and welcome you, but it's been busy. I've been in court all week."

Alex chuckled at the sight of Marley's widening eyes.

"Sadie's a family attorney," he said. "Going to court is her life."

"Oh. I see."

"Nice to meet you, Marley." But Peter was scanning the garden bed. "What *did* happen here?"

Marley straightened her shoulders, looking wary as she removed her gloves. "My chickens happened. I'm sorry. This isn't how I wanted to meet the neighborhood." She offered a tight smile and slipped past Sadie and Peter.

Alex shook his head as she disappeared. "It's a long story."

3

Marley dabbed white acrylic paint beside the yellow splotch then stood back to study her composition with a critical eye. The daisy was bright and happy, the way her followers liked it. Today, her heart wasn't bright and happy. Not when she thought of the five hens spending the night in that truck kennel. They must have been terrified. Still would be.

She'd barely slept for worry about them.

This was why she tried hard not to care about people. Why she didn't even want a pet, though, for the first time in her life, she could have a cat or a dog if she wanted. In a moment of weakness, she'd thought she'd be safe with chickens. They'd supply her with eggs and something to look after. She hadn't expected personalities. She hadn't expected to care.

Not like this.

Her mom had tried to smack her sensitive spirit out of her, but Marley couldn't help who she was. Not only that, but she didn't want to turn into the bitter woman her mother was. To grow old acting like she'd done nothing with her life but suck lemons.

No, there had to be more than that. She'd thought she might find it in religion — so many people seemed to — but that had proved disastrous. Yikes.

Enough.

About this painting. Who wanted daisies, anyway? Blergh.

She parked it on the drying rack next to several other paintings in various degrees of completion, set a fresh canvas in its place, and stared out the window seeking inspiration. The benefit of this roughly pie-shaped corner lot was that she had a terrific view straight down Cedar to the river several blocks below. This property must be worth a mint with a view like that, even though the house leaned a little.

Thank you, Gram Renton.

She'd only met the woman a couple of times, but Gram had run a stream of foster kids through this house in her prime. Dad had been one of those, one of the few who'd come back a couple of times to visit before his untimely death. Gram had remembered and cherished that, but what a shock it had been for Marley to have a deputy show up at her place of work in Yakima to inform her she could claim property in Spokane.

Maybe there really was a God, something Reverend Smith had seriously made her doubt.

Hadn't she told herself enough negative thoughts? She needed to act happy to be happy, but daisies weren't cutting it. Not today.

Marley angled her head and squinted at the blank canvas. A bunch of green leaves. All shapes and shades, like ferns and maybe even beans like the garden next door. What if she painted fewer flowers but added a chicken or two?

Deirdre, in all her Cochin glory. Black downy feathers mottled with white. Fluffy tail. Narrow red comb. Imploring eyes.

Marley held that image in her mind's eye as her hand danced amid shades of green, her entire world narrowed to the twelve-by-twelve canvas on the easel in front of her.

Her doorbell rang, the chime penetrating her creative haze. She stepped back, analyzing the leafy image. It needed a little time to dry before Deirdre took center stage.

The bell rang again. Right. Someone was here. She set her brush down, crossed the room, and opened the door, blinking at the afternoon sunshine. Where had the time gone? The SCRAPS truck sat in her drive again, the officer facing the view down the valley. She hadn't grown up in Marley's neighborhood, that was for sure. A girl never turned her back on the unknown. Although Marley was guilty, too. She hadn't peered through the window to see who was here this time.

"Ms. Riehl?"

The officer turned with a smile. "Hi, Ms. Montgomery. I have good news for you."

"It's Marley, please."

"And I'm Eden. I wanted to let you know that Wesley and Kass Ferguson came through for you. They'll be happy to take your extra chickens. They only live a few blocks from here, and I wondered if you'd like to accompany me to deliver the birds. They'd love to meet you."

Marley took a step back. After yesterday, she hadn't expected an overture of friendship from the animal control officer. And to find her beloved hens would have a happy home... She narrowed her gaze at Eden. "They won't eat them, will they?"

Eden's smile reached her eyes. "They're looking for eggs, not meat birds. Plus their son, Sebastian, is super excited. He's been begging for chickens for a while now."

Marley let the tension drain away. She glanced down at her paint-covered smock. "Give me a minute to clean up, and I'd love to come along."

"Looks like you're painting. I hate to make you leave in the middle—"

"No, it's a good time to let things dry." Marley untied the strings, slipped her arms out of the garment, and draped it over a chair then wrapped her brush. She turned back toward the officer, whose gaze was fixed on the canvases across the space.

"Did you paint those?"

She should step between. Feign ignorance. Deny it. But, no. If she were going to try to earn even a meager living as an artist, she needed to out herself in real life as well as Instagram. She grimaced. It looked nothing like what she saw in her mind, though. Not yet.

"Those leaves look amazing. So detailed. So whimsical."

"I, um..." She took a deep breath. "Thanks. It's not finished." None of them ever were. There was always something that could be improved.

Eden offered another real smile. "I can't wait to see it completed."

That sounded strangely like an offer of friendship. No doubt Marley had misunderstood. She smiled back as she slid her feet into flip flops then reached for the lanyard holding her house key. The neon orange made it easier to keep track of. "Do I need to bring anything else?"

"No, you're good." Eden walked over to the SCRAPS truck while Marley locked up then climbed into the passenger seat.

Eden drove down Cedar, pointing out some of her friends' homes along the way. They turned along the riverside park at the bottom of the hill. "That's where my husband and I live." Eden pointed at a small two-story house flanked with rosebud-loaded bushes. Those might be fun to paint.

Around the curve, she pulled into a driveway and cut the engine. "Here we are. Let's go around back so you can meet them and see the yard before we bring the hens out."

Yesterday Eden had seemed so businesslike. It was probably Marley's fault. Okay, it definitely had been. She must learn to be less impulsive. Fit in better.

Marley looked over the older house as she followed Eden down the sidewalk, through a carport then a gate. A gate meant a fenced yard. That would be good for the birds. She forced herself to relax a little more.

The yard opened up with a wide grassy area surrounded by mature trees. It sloped gently toward the river with a workshop of sorts toward the far end. But before Marley's brain had fully registered the workshop her gaze caught on a life-size bucking bronc made from recycled tools and metal parts.

Her jaw dropped. That creature was amazing. Either these people were wealthy beyond belief or—

A blond man about thirtyish jogged down the steps from the back deck. "Eden!"

"Hi, Wesley. I'd like you to meet Alex and Peter's new

next-door neighbor, Marley Montgomery, previous owner of a few chickens that need rehoming."

Previous owner. Huh. Marley managed a smile. "Nice to meet you. And that mustang... it's crazy wild!" She followed her hunch. "Did you make it?"

He grinned, his gaze flicking over to the huge sculpture and back to her. "Yeah. Like it? It was commissioned by a dude ranch in Montana. It's shipping out next week."

"I've never seen anything like it."

"Marley's a pretty decent artist in her own right." Eden checked her watch. "Do you want to come out to the truck and have a look at the hens?"

"For sure. Let me get Sebastian. He's been dancing out of his skin since I told him what was going on."

A little more stress eased out of Marley. He wouldn't be this nice to a stranger for no reason. No one would be.

A moment later Eden opened the first kennel, and Marley scooped Ginger from its depths. "This is Ginger. She's a Buff Orpington. She really likes to be scratched on her neck."

The boy, who appeared to be about eight years old, beamed as he reached a tentative hand for the hen. "Just like my c-cat, Taz. He likes scratches, too."

It was all Marley could do not to yank Ginger back. "A cat?"

Eden shrugged. "Taz visits the chickens next door all the time. He'll be fine." She looked around. "Kass isn't here? I thought she'd be home by now."

Wesley's face pulled into a frown. "She had to close up the bistro. She and Hailey need to hire more help. Again."

Eden turned to Marley. "Wesley's wife and her cousin

own Bridgeview Bakery and Bistro. You've probably been in there? Great breakfasts and lunches."

"And cinnamon rolls." Sebastian rubbed his tummy.

"My favorite, too." Eden ruffled the boy's hair and grinned at Marley. "Seriously, I've never had better ones."

Marley managed a smile. "I'll have to check them out sometime." As though her budget ran to eating out.

"They display artwork on commission, too." Eden looked thoughtful. "You should definitely show Kass your work. Unless you've got more galleries lined up than you can keep up with."

"But that piece... it's not even finished." How could Eden think it was worth anything? That anyone would even want to own it? Display it?

Wesley lifted the hen from Marley's hands. "I'd love to have a look sometime, if you're up for it."

Marley opened her mouth and snapped it shut again. Was this God's way of showing her this neighborhood of Spokane — Bridgeview — could really be her home? More than a place to live, but with friendly neighbors and everything? But an artist like this man to show any interest in her little hobby... well, he hadn't actually seen her work. He was going by Eden's evaluation, and the animal control officer was just being polite after how yesterday had gone down.

That was it. She was only being nice. Marley'd had little enough of that in her life, and she'd be a fool to take it too seriously. Also a fool not to lap it up.

She reached for the next hen and passed it to Sebastian, who danced a gleeful little jig. Marley turned back to the truck as a man swung off a bicycle beside the carport. She blinked. Alex?

He flashed her a grin as he unbuckled his helmet. "Hey. I came by to see how things were going. I stopped at the bakery and Kass said the big transfer was happening right now."

Sebastian held his Silkie toward the man. "See? She's so soft and pretty."

Alex bumped the boy's shoulder with a gentle fist. "She looks great. What's her name?"

"I-I don't know." The kid frowned and turned back to Marley.

"That's Bianca. She's one of my favorites." Oh, who was she kidding? They were all her favorites. All ten of them. Stupid city regulations, anyway.

They carried the birds into the backyard and set them on the grass. The little flock meandered off to explore their new home while Wesley and Eden discussed what kind of coop he should build. Marley should pay attention. She'd need one herself before winter.

Alex drifted over to Marley. "This seems pretty ideal, don't you think?"

"Thanks for setting it up." Although she'd have preferred non-interference all around.

He shrugged. "Problems are for solving."

But she had to know. "Did you call animal control?"

"What?" He frowned. "You mean in the first place? No. I'd never have done that without talking to you first."

Was he telling the truth? She wasn't that good at reading people. Marley studied his face.

Alex held up both hands. "Promise. I mean, I appreciate laws as much as the next guy..." He must have caught the grimace on her face. "What, you don't like rules? They help society run smoothly."

"Sure they do."

His eyebrows drew together. "Have you read any history, like of the Wild West? Those dudes settled everything with guns. Don't like a guy? Shoot him. Problem solved. Of course, his brothers or friends might retaliate, but that's just how things were."

Marley took a step back, staring at him. "Violence is... evil."

"Laws keep people in check." He shrugged. "When there are repercussions, folks think twice about going on a rampage like that."

How had they got from chickens to murder? This guy was weird. He might have a cute smile, but that's where the attraction ended.

Marley needed to get away from Alex, but she didn't want to come across rude to people who were helping her. She pivoted toward Eden and Wesley, taking a quick look around the backyard. The chickens happily pecked around the the little boy sitting on the grass as he watched them with a wide grin. "Thank you both. I appreciate everything you've done." Minus the interference in the first place. "Looks like everything is under control here. I need to get back up to the house."

"Come visit sometime." Wesley shook her hand with a firm grip.

She gave a half-hearted smile and fled.

4

*A*lex stared after his new neighbor as her long, gathered skirt swept around the corner of the house. Had he caused that? And if so, how? His sister was forever telling him he was putting his foot in his mouth. He turned toward Wesley and Eden. Their faces looked as perplexed as his likely did.

"That was abrupt," Eden commented. "I would have given her a ride back up the hill in a minute."

Alex would have, too, except he'd ridden his bike today. He left his car parked every day that he could, which saved on fuel as well as emissions, plus got him a bit of a workout at the end of the day. That hill wasn't for sissy riders... or walkers. Hmm. It would take Marley a few minutes to hike it.

"I'm heading off, too. I'm glad it all worked out for the chickens to get a new home."

"Thanks for the tip, Alex." Wesley crossed the yard and clouted him on the shoulder. "Much appreciated. Kass and I have been on the fence about whether to jump in now or later, and your call clinched it for us." He grinned at his son. "And Sebastian is going to be a big help for his mama, won't you, buddy? Collecting eggs and everything?"

The little guy pumped his fist. "I will, Daddy."

"Sounds great." Alex waved at Eden. "Thanks for working with Marley, Eden."

"Yeah, no problem." She still looked a little perplexed. "I hope your garden beds recover okay."

"Jasmine thinks they'll be fine."

"Good then."

Alex grabbed his bike's handlebars and looked both directions. Aha, Marley's skirt disappeared around the corner up the hill. He hopped on his bike and pedaled to catch up. Then he coasted alongside her. "Hey."

She glanced over at him. "Hi. You don't need to escort me. I know my way."

Prickly like a porcupine. "I was heading home anyway." He swung his leg over the bar to walk beside her. "No point in me walking half a block behind you, is there?"

She shrugged.

"What did I say to offend you?"

"Nothing."

Alex chuckled. "I'm not buying that."

She blinked rapidly and bit her lip.

What on earth? Tears again? He'd be crazy to hang around this woman at all. Fragile didn't begin to cover her sensitivities. On the other hand, it would take ten minutes to get home, and he wasn't going to let her run him off. Not in his neighborhood. "Where did you live before?"

"Yakima."

"Oh, yeah? All your life?"

Marley crossed her arms over her chest and sped up. "No. And it doesn't matter to you."

"Around Bridgeview, everyone knows their neighbors. It's what makes our community special."

"I suppose you've lived here since birth."

"Guilty as charged." He pointed uphill between two houses. "See that white clapboard? That's my parents' place. My younger brother still lives with them. He's in college." Maybe he was babbling, but if Marley wasn't going to talk, Alex would have to fill the silence. "My oldest brother, Marco, lives over by the school with his wife and their three sons. My next brother, Basil, lives in Seattle." Should he tell her about Basil's DUI and jail time? Naw. She already didn't like Alex. No point in giving her extra reasons. "Then there's my sister Jasmine. She and her husband live a bit further up the hill. They had a baby girl a couple of weeks ago. Lillian Grace."

"That's nice."

Okay, she liked babies. Good to know. "Then there's me. I'm an accountant working my way up to a corner office. And then my kid brother, Evan, who thinks he's smarter than the rest of us and is going into law." He glanced over. "How about you? Siblings?"

"One."

Marley'd break into a jog if she walked any faster. She didn't want to talk. Got it. They turned the corner, and he thumbed toward the long brick building on their right. "That's the Bridgeview Community Center, home of events from cooking clubs to wedding receptions."

Silence.

"Play basketball?" He pointed across the street. "There's often a pick-up game of three-on-three happening in one of those courts. You'd be welcome any time." Although with Hoopfest just around the corner, the guys were pretty focused. Didn't look like Marley would be interested, anyway, since she barely spared a glance.

This had started as a polite gesture to befriend his neighbor, but she was turning it into some sort of challenge. Alex wasn't one to run. He could out-stubborn nearly anyone, with the possible exception of his sister. He swung his bike in front of Marley.

She jerked to a stop, her gaze flying to meet his.

"Am I annoying you? That's not my intention."

"I don't get you."

She could speak. He grinned. "Is a friendly neighbor such a strange concept?"

Marley searched his face. "Tell me about my other neighbor."

Alex sighed. "Kenji Ito. He was a friend of my grandfather's when immigrants first settled this area. I think he worked on the crew that built these bridges." He pointed at the bridge ramp paralleling the street and providing cover for the basketball courts. "His wife passed away maybe ten years ago. They didn't have any kids."

"He seems grumpy."

Now that was the pot calling the kettle black. "He keeps to himself, a rarity in Bridgeview."

Marley pursed her lips, probably wishing Alex would allow her to do the same. Nuh uh. Not on his watch. She shot him a glance. "If it wasn't you who called animal control on me, it must have been him."

Alex held up both hands, and his bike veered against his leg. "It definitely wasn't me. I hadn't been paying attention to how many birds you had. You've got... ah... a lot of cover for them to hide in." Was that diplomatic enough? Because her yard was a disaster.

"So it was *him*, then. Would he think I was bribing him if I took him eggs?"

Alex's eyebrows shot up. "You have extra eggs?"

"Not as many as I had." She scowled. "Will those people really take good care of Bianca and the others?"

"Wesley and Kass? Sure, why not?"

"You'd be surprised. Sometimes the nicest seeming people are mean to animals. Or to anyone helpless."

Another clue. This was a woman who needed understanding. Compassion. "Promise. I've known Kass for a long time. She and Wesley have been married maybe a year? No, a bit less, I think. I don't keep track."

"The boy is his? They look too much alike for that not to be true."

Alex nodded. "Wesley was divorced and then his ex died so he suddenly had full custody."

"He didn't before? There's usually a reason."

Seriously? Marley was going there? "Women are more likely to get custody, from what I hear. But, whatever. Wesley's a good guy. He's not going to go around kicking chickens, if that's what you're worried about."

⌒ ᴸ ᶜ

AT LEAST SHE'D managed to quiet him for the last couple of blocks home. Maybe he was angry that she might have thought his friend could have a mean streak. A girl couldn't be too careful, and she'd never willingly put her hens in danger. At least she could keep an eye on them, knowing where they lived. That was better than them disappearing into the unknown. But then she'd grieve once and get it done instead of always wondering.

She stared at the medley of leaves she'd painted earlier then dabbed her brush into white paint. She blocked out the shape of a cartoonish chicken. Then another one, their heads close together. All the details of the painting took shape in her mind, and it needed to be created *now*. She pointed her hair dryer at the canvas until it was dry enough for the next color.

Two hours later she painted the final stroke and set down her brush. She massaged her hands together and bent one way then the other to loosen the crick in her back. But the painting was her finest yet. Bianca and Deirdre had come to life — or the kind of life they'd have as whimsical caricatures with expressive eyes and faces.

Maybe she could sell paintings like this. In the glow of evening light coming in from her north-facing window, she shot a few photos with her phone and uploaded the best one to Instagram. She'd always envisioned being an artist, but the mundane realities of food and shelter had kept her dream at bay until now. With a rent-free place to live and a small garden to help feed her, maybe it could become reality.

How would she even go about selling them, though? An Etsy shop? Because she couldn't take time to have booths at craft fairs or other events. She liked people well enough, but an artist needed to create, not meet the public all the time.

What had Eden said? Bridgeview Bakery and Bistro displayed artwork for sale. Maybe Marley would pay them a visit and see what kind of vibe the place had. The cheerful awnings over outdoor seating looked welcoming, and the place seemed crowded every time she went past. Definitely worth a shot.

Her stomach growled, and she realized she hadn't eaten for seven or eight hours. That was no way to take care of herself, but she needed to get some groceries. Looked like another omelet night if the girls had produced more eggs since she'd last checked.

Marley hung her smock and headed into the backyard. Deirdre and Zephyr came running, Chloe not far behind. Marley crouched to give them all some love. She checked their water and feeder then made the rounds of their hiding spots. In a few minutes she had four eggs tucked into the turned-up hem of her T-shirt.

Her elderly neighbor sat on his back porch, rocking and studying her.

"Hi." She might as well be friendly. After all, she'd met the guys on the other side, and no one had bitten her yet.

The old man dipped his head in acknowledgment.

"Would you like some eggs?" she blurted. Okay, so she'd have to scrounge for something else to eat, but it was more important to make friends with the neighbor. "I just picked up a few fresh ones."

The rocker sped up. "No, thank you."

"Are you sure? There will be more tomorrow. I'm happy to share."

He shook his head.

"I'm Marley Montgomery. Gram Renton used to be my dad's foster mom. I suppose you knew her well."

He nodded, but his eyes narrowed.

It occurred to Marley that he was treating her like she'd treated Alex a few hours ago. So this was what it felt like to work for every bit of conversation. She shouldn't have been so cold to Alex. His talk of Old West shootings likely didn't mean anything.

"Okay, well, have a great evening." Marley gathered her hem tightly in one hand and opened her door with the other.

Aromas of grilling steak from the other house caught her attention, and she glanced over to see Peter and Sadie wrapped in each other's arms, kissing away near the barbecue. Then their voices murmured, low, and Sadie laughed softly. She leaned against Peter as he turned back to check their dinner.

Marley let herself into the house and closed the door quietly. It would never do to be thought of as a snoopy neighbor. She set the eggs in a bowl then pulled the stained gingham curtain across the sink window so she wouldn't be tempted to sneak another peek. Ugh. She also needed to do the dishes before she could fix the omelet.

She had more in common with Kenji Ito than the people closer to her age in the other house. They had family. Busy lives. Romance.

Well, maybe not Alex. Surely, he'd have mentioned if he were dating or engaged like his cousin. He'd talked so much it would have come out. So he was unattached for now, but it likely wouldn't last long. An accountant with what sounded like a good job, his own home, a thriving business with his family around him. Yeah. That guy had it made.

Unlike Marley. Winning Mrs. Renton's favor was the first break she'd ever had. And maybe the painting drying on the rack in the other room. With any luck at all, she could forge her own future from here.

A man to support her was a complication she didn't need.

5

*S*he's not out in her yard?" Peter's voice was laced with amusement.

Alex glared at his cousin from over by the kitchen sink and held up a bowl dripping with soap suds. "Hello, ever heard of washing dishes?"

"Sure have. I've done a few myself, but you're distracted. You keep leaning to look out the window toward next door."

"Do not." Alex rinsed the dish and slotted it into the drain rack. "I was just checking on the bean plants in that garden bed the chickens tore through. They look like they're recovering okay."

Peter bellowed a laugh. "Since when do you care about every single bean plant?"

"I'm hurt." He dropped the cutlery into the sink with a splash. "Of course, I care. Every plant contributes to the business's bottom line, so, as your financial advisor, it matters to me."

"And Jasmine and I appreciate it." Peter planted both

hands on the counter and peered out the window at a deep angle.

Alex hadn't been that obvious, had he? No, of course not. His cousin was exaggerating to make a point. Alex flicked suds at Peter. "Excuse me. You're blocking the faucet."

"Oh, I beg your pardon." But he didn't move. "Looks like she's been digging up that back section by hand. That's some dedication."

"I noticed." No. Why hadn't he kept his mouth shut?

Peter grinned as he eased back from the window. "I thought you might have caught sight of that in one of your three hundred casual glances over there. So, you gonna make a move on our neighbor?"

Deflection. That would be the best plan. "Just because you're engaged to the woman who lives on the west side doesn't mean I need to follow in your footsteps."

"You've got to admit it's convenient." Peter grabbed a clean dish towel from the drawer and picked up a bowl. "I get to move into a great heritage house with a lush back-yard. Sadie's patio is an awesome relaxing spot with that little fountain. Beats looking at a row of sterile garden beds. Beats living with *you*."

Alex narrowed his gaze at his cousin. "I'd like to remind you that the sterile garden beds, as you put it, are for *your* business. I'm allowing the takeover of my space as part of my contribution to Bridgeview Backyards. It's mostly you who keeps them weed-free."

"And I appreciate it. I do. But you've got to admit, it's not such a relaxing space. There's not even a tree on the property."

"Trees drop leaves that need raking, to say nothing of

providing too much shade for a lot of vegetables. You know that."

Peter set the bowl in the cupboard and reached for another. "Yes, but, dude, there's more to life than vegetables. Sadie had the right idea when she bought Mrs. Essery's house, creating an oasis from the stresses of everyday life. Now, granted, I had my eye on that property myself. Had my own vision for it. Can I just say I like how it turned out, though? A nice balance. The raspberry canes stayed, and we've got a nice little area where we can grow a few greens and radishes and a tomato plant or two, but not so big that it takes over the entire yard."

"Because all the vegetables are being grown next door, where you have easy access." Alex glared at his cousin. "You seem to have conveniently forgotten how you and me and Jasmine hammered out the details of how and where to grow the produce you were going to sell."

"Don't forget Basil."

Alex grunted. Yeah, his older brother had been part of the business for a while, too. Until he'd been arrested and the rest of them had been forced to buy him out so he could pay his fines. "That's not the point. The point is that you hate my yard, and yet it's become exactly what you wanted it to be. You think I'd have it this way if it weren't for Bridgeview Backyards?"

Peter raised his eyebrows but didn't speak as he grabbed a handful of cutlery.

"It will be just like Nonna's yard when it matures. Wasn't that the goal? A space packed with growing things and food for a family or two?" In the case of the Santoro matriarch, enough for five families, but Nonna didn't seem able to stop planting and puttering though she'd be eighty this fall.

"Defensive much? Nonna's yard is a little less perfect. More evolved." Spoons clattered into the drawer.

"Who's to say my yard won't evolve? This is our third summer. Doesn't evolution take millions of years?"

"Nonna's not *that* old." Peter chuckled. "Sorry I'm stomping on your toes. That's not my intention. I was only commenting that Marley seems nice enough and she's got some grit, digging up part of her rocky yard. Though that mass of bushes and flowers has its own wild kind of beauty."

So did Marley.

The thought came unbidden, but Alex pushed it aside. He wasn't looking for a girlfriend. Not now, anyway. He would earn his promotion by the time he was thirty. Then he'd be in a better position to provide for a wife. There was no point in dating for the fun of it. A guy shouldn't mess with random emotions. His own... or hers.

Marley definitely wasn't the right kind of woman for him, anyway. She had issues. A messy past... and he didn't even know if she followed Jesus. That was important. Plus, Alex had learned his lesson about trying to rescue damsels in distress a few years ago when he'd actually proposed to Linnea Ranta. He still couldn't believe he'd blurted out the words, risking his entire future because his high school crush was in a tight spot. He cared about her, sure, but he hadn't been in love. Even then he'd seen her falling for Logan Dermott, and it killed him the other guy was such a jerk. Alex had only wanted to rescue her.

That wasn't love. Since then he'd watched Jasmine fall in love with Nathan then Peter with Sadie. Other friends, too, but he'd had a front row seat to his sister's and his cousin's romances. He shuddered slightly. He'd had a narrow escape with Linnea. What if she'd been desperate enough to agree? Would they have come to love each other, or would they have already become a divorce statistic?

Alex was older now. Wiser, by far, and also a wee bit leery. He'd keep pushing any thoughts of love off into the distant, hazy future.

"Oh, there she is now."

He leaned toward the window then caught Peter's guffaw. He skewered his cousin with a glare, but his cousin only laughed harder. Alex scooped an entire handful of suds at Peter, who danced away, snapping his dish towel at Alex's legs.

The battle was on. And Alex hadn't even caught a glimpse of the pretty girl next door.

SHE WAS LONELY.

Not only had Marley never been enough for her mom or even her dad — though he'd tried — she wasn't even enough for herself. To top it off, her yard was less of an oasis than she'd hoped.

Kenji Ito spent a crazy amount of time sitting on his back porch watching her, like he was waiting for her to break another law so he could report her again.

And that's why she'd worked outside at the crack of dawn strapping bamboo poles to the old picket fence that lined the walkway between their houses and attaching a roll of mesh from the hardware store along it. Next time he went inside, she'd poke runner bean seeds into the ground every few inches. She hadn't had a chance to do a good job digging up the grass or fertilizing the soil, but with any luck, a lot of the seeds would sprout.

She'd need a better plan by next year. Or maybe she could win the old guy over.

Nah. He was creepy.

The spot she'd chosen for the rest of her vegetables was closer to the other side, but digging up the area was hard work. The dirt seemed thicker over there, but there were so many stones, which shouldn't be this much of a surprise considering the rocky slope that angled steeply upward beyond the rickety pickets. She'd been unable to resist a wooden planter with bright annuals for beside her steps. Raised beds were likely the best plan for her entire yard.

Not this year, though. They'd be so expensive. For now, Marley dug while the paint dried. By alternating between the two activities, she had a row of twelve square canvases with her chickens staring whimsically out of them. They were pretty good, if she did say so herself.

She was certifiable... and needed out of the house before she put words to Gloria's incessant clucking. But was she ready to show someone else her work in real life? Just based on the animal control officer's offhand comment about a leaf-covered canvas and a bunch of hearts on Instagram?

It was either try to sell her paintings or get a job, and she didn't have much experience beyond waitressing. A job would give her a much-needed people fix and a bit of steady income, but there wasn't much within easy walking distance besides the bistro and a swanky-looking Italian restaurant.

Marley packed her social media followers' three favorite paintings into her portfolio case, changed into her nicest skirt and blouse, and tried to do something with her mass of wavy hair. She was out of her favorite product that helped tame it. Yes, a real paying job would be a good idea. But then she'd probably need a car, and that cost money, too. She did the best she could with her hair, grabbed her canvas backpack purse and the portfolio, and stepped out the front door before she lost her nerve.

What a glorious June afternoon! Marley dodged a puddle left from last night's rain and inhaled fresh and fragrant air. The houses on either side of the street each had a unique style, yet were somehow unified by flowerbeds bursting from their front yards.

An old woman stared out of a picture window halfway down the hill. Marley lifted a hand to wave, and the woman returned the gesture. Maybe if she'd been this proactive with Kenji, her grumpy neighbor wouldn't have reported her to animal protection.

Marley strode around the L-shaped yellow-and-white striped awning that shaded small round tables. She pulled open the bistro's heavy glass door and stepped inside to an upbeat, happy space. Whitewashed planks covered the walls, and nearly half of the wooden tables were surrounded by chattering, laughing people seated on brightly painted chairs.

Best of all was the aroma of cinnamon rolls that assaulted her, just like young Sebastian had said. She spied several of the large delicacies sitting in a turquoise glass-fronted case. Could she afford one? And maybe a cup of tea? It would look better if she were a paying customer and not just someone out to sell them stuff, right?

Right.

Marley clutched her portfolio in front of her and approached the counter.

A largely pregnant redhead turned to offer her a tired smile. "Good afternoon."

"Hi, my name is Marley Montgomery, and I'm new to the neigh—"

The woman's face brightened. "The chicken lady?"

"Um..."

"Sorry. I'm Kass Ferguson, and I wasn't home when you and Eden brought the hens by last week. That *was* you, wasn't it?"

Marley blinked. "Yes." She shifted the portfolio. "I hope they're settling in well."

"They are. And Sebastian is as big a help as he promised to be, making sure they have fresh water. He collects the eggs, too."

"That's great."

"Eden mentioned you were an artist. I hope you've got something in that bag to show me."

Wow. Just... wow. "I do, if you've got a minute." Marley glanced around the space. "But it looks like you might be pretty busy."

"I need to get off my feet."

A short, thin, older woman came around the counter carrying a coffee pot. Kass touched her arm. "Astrid, can I get you to watch the counter for a few minutes before you head out?"

"Certainly." Astrid cast a curious glance at Marley then began offering refills to the patrons.

Kass turned to Marley. "Would you like a cup of tea while we talk? I need one in the worst way."

"That sounds wonderful." Marley pulled her purse from off her back. "And I'd love to try a cinnamon roll, please. I've heard rave reviews about them."

"Put your wallet away. It's on the house today. Maybe I can bribe you into doing business with us. Find a table, and I'll join you in a minute."

Unexpected. She made her way to a vacant table by the window, unlatched her portfolio, and stacked the paintings off to the side before taking a seat on a yellow chair and looking around again. She could see her chickens happily displayed here. Groupings of birds and cats made of nuts and bolts graced several shelves across the space. Wesley's work on a smaller scale? And then another section with rustic pottery plates.

Maybe this could work. But how much would they be able to move? Did tourists come to this bistro off the beaten track? She might need another venue or two.

Kass set a small tray down and off-loaded two teacups and a plated cinnamon roll. The tantalizing fragrance of cinnamon and brown sugar tickled Marley's nostrils. If that thing was half as tasty as it smelled, she'd be in heaven for a few minutes.

Astrid swept by and gathered the empty tray while Kass took a seat with a heartfelt sigh. "We so badly need more help around here. I'm not sure how my cousin will manage the business when I'm off with the baby." She eyed Marley as she took a sip of her tea. "You're not looking for a job, are you?"

Marley started to shake her head but stopped. Did she or didn't she? Maybe it depended on how well her art sold. "Not at the moment."

"It was too much to hope for." Kass lifted the top painting and examined it before raising her eyebrows at Marley. "This is the original?"

"Well, yes." What else would it be?

"I was expecting prints. You'd get a lot more mileage out of each hour spent painting if you went that route."

"I..." The thoughts trailed off as heat crept up her cheeks. "I haven't really figured that part out yet." How much would it cost? She had enough of an investment in canvases and paints. How could she afford to get prints made and still eat? She couldn't. Not now.

"Don't get me wrong. These are great. I think they'll be popular. I just hate to see you burn yourself out on one-offs." Kass held up a painting at arm's length and squinted at it. "I'd totally hang these on the wall over there, and I'll buy one for the house, too. They're so cheerful and fun. I think I'd like one in the baby's room."

Marley blinked. "Really? That's... awesome." She pulled the bottom canvas out of the stack. "This one is of Bianca."

Kass laughed as she took it from Marley's hands. "Oh, wow. You captured her personality so well. I'll take it. How many does that leave for the bistro?"

"I have a dozen completed in this style."

"Awesome. Let's agree on a commission and delivery time. I'll get Wesley to arrange them in a block. Except, wait, there are only eleven, since I'm taking Bianca home."

"I can have another one completed tomorrow."

Kass's face brightened as she pulled herself to her feet. "Perfect. Now you eat up that cinnamon roll while I go dig out a copy of our standard artist contract."

Several men in suits and ties came through the door, laughing, talking, and swinging briefcases.

Kass shook her head and glanced back at Marley. "Looks like my break is over, since Astrid's off the clock at three. Are you *sure* you don't want a job? Even part time?"

*a*lex followed his coworkers in the door at Bridgeview Bakery and Bistro. Man, the place was hopping today. He grinned at the sight of his dad at a table in the corner with his brothers, all three talking over each other and gesturing wildly, but the smile faded when he remembered big, bold Uncle Alberto would never join them again. Had he really been gone nearly two years?

Think about something else.

Was that Marley with her back to the door, sitting alone? Sure looked like her crazy hair. And what was on the table beside her? The angle was wrong to see clearly. Hey, he'd grab his coffee and join her. Why not? Be friendly. Neighborly. He'd see Nelson and Clint at the office again in the morning.

A minute later he stopped beside her table, black coffee in hand. "Hey, Marley. Mind if I join you?"

She looked up from the spiral notebook in front of her, pen poised over the page. "Um, hi. Sure. That would be fine." She dragged a plate with a half-eaten cinnamon roll closer to make room.

Alex settled into the chair across from her and gestured around the space. "I see you've found our local watering hole. And discovered their signature pastries."

"It's a great space, and the cinnamon roll is amazing."

He let his gaze drift to the stack of canvases beside her elbow. Right, she'd told him she was an artist, but this? The eyes of a garish upside-down chicken seemed focused on his. Whoa. He nodded toward it and looked at Marley. "Your work?"

Her face lit up, and her blue eyes sparkled. "Yes! And the owner here, Kath—"

"Kass," he corrected.

"Oh, right. Kass. She wants to display them here for sale. I'm so excited right now I can hardly contain myself."

Kass wanted crazy poultry eyes staring at everyone who came in here? Maybe they looked better right side up. He reached toward the canvases. "May I?"

She bit her lip but nodded, her gaze watchful.

So she was worried what he'd think, or maybe she'd already read his expression and found it lacking in enthusiasm. He tried for a more genuine smile as he turned the paintings right side up and shuffled through them. They didn't look like any chickens he'd ever met with their elongated necks and over-sized eyes, but they couldn't be anything else. And, while they weren't exactly his style, he could see the strokes had a sort of mastery about them. Even those uncanny eyes.

He glanced at her. "You're a good artist." That, at least, he could say with sincerity.

"You really think so?" Marley's eyes brightened.

"Yeah. They're so... colorful." Also weird, but he wasn't saying that out loud.

"Bright colors make me happy."

Bright colors made Alex want to flinch and hide. He liked his suits navy, his T-shirts gray, and his walls cream. Restful. According to his sister, also maybe a little stuffy and boring, but he didn't mind.

A shadow fell over the table as a hand gripped Alex's shoulder. "Off the clock so early today?"

He looked up into his dad's eyes. "We worked through lunch. Big deadline, but we hit it."

"Good job." Dad glanced at Marley then flicked his eyebrows at Alex, just a smidge. And Dad's brothers hovered on either side, expressions alive with curiosity.

Alex sighed. He was never going to hear the end of this. Italians loved romance, and Mom and Nonna had been ganging up on him lately. Apparently, it was his turn to find love, and no amount of explaining he wasn't planning to look around until he turned thirty made them stop. A report of this meeting would spread through his family like wildfire.

"Dad, this is my next-door neighbor, Marley. I ran into her here just now *by accident*."

Dad's eyes twinkled.

"Marley, my father, Ray Santoro. He's a commercial pilot, and apparently he's not flying today."

Dad reached for Marley's hand and pressed his lips to the back of it. "I am so pleased to meet you, Marley. Are you Mabel Renton's granddaughter?"

Marley tugged her hand free as a flush crept up her face.

She sent a plaintive glance at Alex. "It's a bit more complicated than that."

Right. That whole foster parent thing. Alex might as well get the entire production over with. He thumbed toward one sidekick. "This is my uncle Dino Santoro. He's in construction. And over here we have my uncle Franco, an electrician. They were just leaving."

Not by the grin Uncle Dino sent him. "Nice to meet you. My wife and I have heard all about you from our son, Peter."

Dad turned to Dino. "You have? And yet your son is engaged to be married, and my very single son has mentioned nothing to his mamma or to mine. Now, I have been away for a few days, it's true, but I'm sure Grace would have mentioned something to me if Alex had uttered a single word."

Mom definitely would have fired a text for Dad to receive whenever he landed, and then they'd have talked about the possibilities at length on the phone. In Italian. Mom would not let a pretty young woman slip away without careful consideration.

Wait. Marley was attractive? Alex studied her for a few seconds as she smiled awkwardly at Dino, her face pinker than usual. Yeah, she was pretty, but not in a classic way. Not a blond beauty like Linnea or a stunning redhead like Kass. Marley was less conventional, both in her wild hair and how she dressed. Still, strangely captivating.

"Welcome to Bridgeview, then, Miss Marley," Dad went on. "Did you have friends here before you moved?"

She shook her head. "I didn't know a soul, sir."

"Well, we must remedy that. Come for Sunday dinner."

Had Alex managed to keep his groan inward?

"I'll tell my wife to set an extra plate. It's no trouble, and we won't take no for an answer. You can walk over with Alex after church. The beauty of Bridgeview is that everything is within a few blocks."

"After... church?" Her wide eyes shifted to Alex.

"My family attends Bridgeview Bible Church. You might have seen it up the side street behind the bistro. I usually cut across from Cedar to save a few blocks."

Marley looked back at Dad. "Thank you for your kind offer."

The three Santoro men all wore identical grins. Sort of like cats who'd found an overturned cream pitcher... or like hens who dust-bathed enthusiastically in someone else's garden.

Dad patted Marley's shoulder. "See you Sunday." He headed out the door, his brothers following.

That had been awkward. "Look, don't let my dad bully you. If you have other plans, that's fine."

"What is your church like?"

Alex blinked. Instead of worrying about his family trying to matchmake him, he should be concerned about Marley's soul.

꩜

THAT GLEAM in Ray Santoro's eyes had been just as obvious as the discomfort oozing from Alex's. Her next-door neighbor had stopped at her table to be polite. He didn't like her chickens. He didn't like her paintings. He didn't like *her*. At least not in the way his father and uncles seemed to think.

Family drama. Looked like a totally different kind of it

than what Marley had grown up with. Likely Alex's clan would change their mind about her when they got to know her. Right now, they were just curious.

She was curious, too. What was a big family like? Alex had four siblings, and it looked like his father also came from a large family. She couldn't even imagine.

"It's a great church."

Marley had nearly forgotten she'd asked.

"About one-fifty to two hundred attendees most weeks. Lots of kids. People of all ages, really. Pastor Tomas Ramirez is a terrific guy who loves Jesus and loves people, and it shows."

"That sounds... appealing." No one could ever have commended Reverend Smith that way. The razor-thin, sharp-eyed man was known more as a hellfire-and-brimstone kind of preacher. He'd tried to scare Marley into the kingdom, first one way, then another.

Spokane was a long way from Yakima, and Alex's pastor sounded very different from Reverend Smith. The God she'd read about in the Bible sounded more like a God of love. But, was He? "What is your God like?"

Alex blinked and leaned back in his chair, studying her. At least he seemed to take the question seriously. "Hard to describe in a few sentences, but here goes. He's the Creator of the universe and everything in it. He created humans to be His companions, to worship Him. Only He gave us free will, and so lots of us went our own way, ignoring Him. Avoiding Him."

Marley nodded cautiously.

"So, Jesus is God. That part's a little complicated, but like ice and steam are both just water but in different environments, Jesus is one aspect of God. He came to Earth to demonstrate God's love and to die for us, to redeem us, to bring humanity back into a relationship with Him."

That cleared up a few things. "So God loves us? He doesn't punish us for the bad stuff we do?" Reverend Smith was big on the judgment angle.

Alex took a sip of his coffee and leaned closer, his elbows on the table. "Yes and no. The Bible calls the bad stuff sin. It's us rebelling against God. He loves us and doesn't want to discipline us, but if we don't ask forgiveness and acknowledge the redemption He's offered, He will have no choice but to punish us at the end of time."

Punish. Echoes of Reverend Smith. Marley shuddered. "That's a lot to take in." Maybe he'd been partly right.

"Yeah, sorry. I'm sure there are clearer ways to explain it all, but that's kind of the Cliff Notes version. Pastor Tomas is better at this kind of stuff than I am."

"Thanks. It gives me something to think about." Time to think was one of the benefits of her new lifestyle. Or possibly a drawback, depending on the day.

"Church starts at ten-thirty. I usually leave the house at ten-fifteen, if you want to walk over together."

He was only being polite. "No, that's okay. I'll go on my own." And find a seat at the back where she could escape if things turned uncomfortable.

Alex nodded. "My dad meant the dinner invitation. You up for it? It's a way to meet a bunch of the neighborhood in one go."

Marley studied his face. "Your dad seems to think..."

He chuckled, but looked away. "Hazards of a large family. My grandmother has decided it's my turn, but I'm not interested." Alex's gaze shot to meet hers. "Wait, that came out wrong. I mean, I have goals for my life and eventually want to get married, but not anytime soon, no matter what Nonna says." He rubbed his neck. "I am messing this up. Badly."

She chuckled. At least she knew where she stood. "Same with me. Marriage is a possible eventuality, but I'm not on a manhunt."

He visibly relaxed then drained his coffee cup. "Well, so long as we are on the same page, that's great. I hope you'll come to dinner."

"Thanks. I'd like that. Cooking for one person gets old." She held up both hands. "And that sounded manhuntish. Sorry."

Alex laughed. "No, I get it. Although I usually have a houseful. Right now there's just me and Peter, but a friend of a guy I work with is moving in soon. He's a pilot for an outdoor adventure company. My friends Logan and Linnea just moved back from Edmonds, so my suite is rented out, too. They'll be looking for a place to buy at some point, but for now they've got the basement."

"Sounds like a busy place." And it explained all the vehicles coming and going.

"Yeah, it is. I like it that way."

Marley would, too. She'd spent far too much time by herself lately. The hens were great company, but not so conversational. What would it be like to have a cousin she was close to like Alex and Peter? Or even just a roommate? But her house was so tiny. The second bedroom was small and still packed with Gram Renton's junk. Plus, the entire living room was taken up with Marley's studio. No, she wouldn't be bringing in a roommate anytime soon, no matter how tired she got of her own company or how helpful the income would be.

Alex glanced in his empty coffee cup then looked around. "Want a refill?"

She blinked. Her tea was tepid. A bit more hot water wouldn't go amiss. "That sounds good."

He rose and strode over to the counter. He said something to Kass, who was plating cookies for a man with three little kids, then plucked a carafe with hot water from the coffee machine. He poured for Marley then exchanged the pot for one filled with coffee, poured himself a cup then made the rounds of other customers, topping up a dozen mugs around the bistro.

Huh.

She dunked her teabag in the hot water and nibbled a bit more of that luscious cinnamon roll while trying not to watch Alex as he chatted with various patrons. Finally he parked the carafe, dumped out the filter, and started a new pot before patting the owner on the shoulder. Kass gave him a relieved smile.

Okay, Marley was staring now. The guy seemed to know his way around here... but then, this was Bridgeview, and his actions lined up with everything he'd said about it being a tight community. One she wanted to stay part of.

Kass had pretty much offered Marley a job twice while they talked about paintings. She clearly needed help if this scenario was what it seemed. And that was not even counting the fact that the owner would soon need to take time off with a new baby.

This was obviously a popular hangout with many regulars, and within easy walking distance of Marley's house. A part-time job would be kind of fun. She'd get out and meet people while still having lots of time for gardening and painting.

She wasn't created for a solitary life.

7

*M*arley stood by the huge window in the church foyer, watching as Pastor Tomas greeted a line of people. He took a moment to shake every hand, look in people's eyes, and exchange a few words. The laugh lines around his mouth and crinkles around his eyes proved that this man smiled often.

He was *so* not Reverend Smith.

The older woman who'd waved to Marley the other day pressed the pastor's hand between both of hers and leaned in to kiss the air on either side of his face.

"Nice to see you, Marietta. How are you keeping?"

"Good, good. You know my grandson Antonio is living with me now. My sons think I need a keeper."

Pastor Tomas chuckled. "Be nice to the poor lad, Marietta. With his new restaurant just getting off the ground, I'm sure he's not under your feet much."

"It is true. And he is a good boy." She leaned closer and lowered her voice. "Did you know that our Alex has met someone?"

Marley's ears perked up. This was Alex's nonna? Only a few days ago, Alex had said he wasn't looking for a girlfriend. Wow, talk about a fast mover.

"He has?"

The older woman nodded firmly. "I'm going to dinner at Raimondo and Grazia's to meet her. She is an artist."

Raimondo? Ray. Wait... artist? No way. Alex's grandmother thought Marley was the someone special in Alex's life? He *had* warned her his mom and grandma were focused on his lack of love life.

At least Marley had this bit of forewarning, if she'd needed it after meeting Alex's dad and uncles with their unabashed curiosity. Obviously, no one had overheard the part of her conversation with Alex where they agreed they could be friends because neither was looking for more.

She sighed.

Through the open doors of the sanctuary, a group of guys and girls around her own age laughed and talked together, slowly moving toward the foyer. Alex was in the midst. He tipped his head back and laughed, a sound that wafted over the other congregants' chatter.

He was easy to look at with his short dark hair, striking blue eyes, and strong face with its ready smile and a hint of a dimple in his left cheek. When the time came, he'd be a great catch for some lucky woman.

Alex's gaze snapped onto hers from thirty feet away, and he grinned.

Marley felt a little jolt in her heart. Uh, no. That blip was not welcome here. Neighbors. Neighbors and maybe friends. That was all, and it was more than enough. She wasn't in any position to pursue more. She didn't even want to.

He excused himself from his friends and made his way toward her. "You made it! I didn't see you here."

She'd seen *him*. "I sat by the doors."

"Hey, that's cool." Alex rocked back on his heels. "Ready to go? Or would you like me to introduce you around here?"

He'd said he had a big family. That might be enough faces to keep straight for one day. She mustered a smile. "I'm ready to leave."

"Sure." He waved at the pastor then placed his hand on the small of Marley's back to guide her out the door.

Not that she needed escorting. The doors were propped open to the June sunshine, a view of the river below visible between nearby buildings. But when was the last time a guy had given her the courtesy of that sort of gentlemanly touch? Since — she tried to think — never.

His hand dropped away as they descended the steps, and he pointed out the sidewalk between two houses, connecting the parking lot to Cedar Street.

She nodded. She'd found the shortcut earlier, thanks to his tip.

"What did you think of Bridgeview Bible?" He shoved both hands in his pants pockets and glanced at her.

Marley chewed her lip. "Really different from the church I sometimes went to before. I liked it, though."

"Pastor Tomas has a way of making me think."

"I can see why. He seems very down to earth." The sermon series he'd announced was about the attributes of God. Although Pastor Tomas had talked about God being omniscient — all-knowing — he'd taken a different tack than Reverend Smith would have. That man would have speared each person with a stern look and an admonition to clean up their act so God wouldn't hate them too much. She shuddered.

"You okay?"

He'd noticed? Marley glanced up at Alex, close by her side on the narrow walkway. "Yeah. Just had a chill." Reverend Smith's shadow would cause one any day of the year.

Alex told her something about the people who lived in every house they passed, not that she'd remember any of it later. They crossed beneath the bridge, the basketball courts silent as they went by, and turned into the drive of a large but unpretentious white house.

"Ready?" he asked.

Not hardly. Marley gave a little shrug.

He brushed her arm as he reached for the knob. "Don't let them pressure you. We know where we stand with each other." He winked and pushed the door open.

Friend zone. Exactly where she wanted him. Right?

WHAT DID she think of the craziness? To Alex, the hubbub was a normal part of being Santoro. His nephew Oren popped around the corner from the hallway. "They're here!" he yelled.

The voices and laughter ended abruptly, a baby's wail breaking the sudden silence. Then Alex's family flowed from the kitchen into the family room. Arie launched his ninja moves at Alex. Grabbing his six-year-old nephew and tickling him was a welcome distraction.

Dad appeared in the patio doors, open to the back deck,

allowing aromas of grilling meat to waft into the house. "Marley! You are welcome here."

"Thank you."

Alex glanced over at her quiet response. This must be wildly overwhelming to her.

Nonna pushed her way through and stood surveying Marley. "You are Marley? The artist?"

"I am."

"I am Marietta. You have met Raimondo, si? He is my firstborn. Grazia, where are you?" Nonna pulled Alex's mom beside her. "This is Raimondo's wife, Grazia. Marco is their firstborn, and here is his wife Daria. They have three boys. Stair-steppers Caden and Oren and Arie."

Alex leaned toward Marley. "They're a wild bunch."

She gave him a fleeting smile.

"Jasmine is Raimondo's daughter, and this is her husband, Nathan. And this wee one is their daughter, Lillian, my newest great-grandchild. So precious."

Did Marley love babies? All women seemed to go gaga over them. Alex was rather besotted with his sister's infant himself.

"She's lovely," Marley offered.

Nonna seemed satisfied. "Alex you have met. And over there is Evan, the youngest. He goes to the university. That is all."

Evan said hi, offering Alex a knowing smirk. Hadn't Alex made it clear to his kid brother that Dad had pushed this situation? And now Nonna was taking over.

Nonna beckoned Marley. "Come see the baby."

Marley took a hesitant step forward, glancing at Alex like she feared losing him in this turmoil. Well, he'd promised to be her friend. He couldn't very well abandon her.

Alex took baby Lillian from his brother-in-law. He'd held her enough times that it didn't feel *too* awkward anymore. He angled her toward Marley. "My niece," he said proudly.

"She's so tiny."

"Only two weeks old."

"Wow." She stroked the baby's tiny fist but made no effort to lift Lillian from his arms.

That was fine. He didn't mind holding her longer.

Jasmine edged closer. "Hi, Marley. I'm Alex's sister, Jasmine, in case you missed it. I've heard a lot about you."

Alex gave his sister a sharp look. Whatever she'd heard hadn't been from him. Either Peter or Sadie had been speaking out of turn. Or maybe they hadn't said anything incriminating. He could hope.

Jasmine grinned at him as she pressed Marley's hand. "Come on and have a seat. My mom has booted me out of the kitchen, anyway. Apparently, I am fragile from childbirth." She laughed. "Everyone else will get food on the table while we get to know each other."

There was no reason for her words to sound ominous. Marley was new to the neighborhood and wanted to get to meet people. This was a perfect opportunity. In fact, Alex should simply trust his sister and walk away. Take baby Lillian out to the back deck where Dad was grilling — Alex's thoughts stuttered — chicken.

Oh, no. Was Marley vegetarian? The way she went on about her birds, she probably didn't eat meat, especially not poultry. Would she simply pass the platter, or would she denounce his entire family and storm from the house? Why hadn't he thought about this in advance? Warned his parents? And Nonna. While Mom and Dad might handle the situation tactfully, Nonna was more likely to speak her mind bluntly. It wouldn't be pretty.

"Joining us, Alex?" Jasmine settled into a corner of the loveseat as Marley perched on the edge of the chair kitty-corner to her.

"Uh..." Alex jiggled the baby, who arched her back as she stretched, both hands fisted tightly. Whom should he warn? Dad? Mom? Or maybe Marley. Surely, she could handle herself. If she didn't eat meat, she had to be accustomed to politely declining. The memory of her overwrought tears a couple of weeks ago tugged at his senses. If he could avoid a repeat, he'd do that. "I'm going to check in with Dad."

"Okay." Jasmine gave him an odd look. For that matter, so did Marley.

Whatever. They could have their girl-talk and he'd get out of their way. He shifted Lillian to his shoulder and strolled toward the patio doors. Thankfully, the men had headed out there while the women retreated to the kitchen. By the irregular thumping sound from outside, his nephews bounced a basketball around on the paved driveway.

"Hey, a baby looks good on you." Marco lifted a glass of wine and grinned at Alex as he came through the door.

"She's pretty cute when she's asleep."

Nathan chuckled. "Agreed on that. She's having trouble getting night and day figured out, though. Could sure use a solid night's sleep sometime soon."

"We should practice some three-on-three after lunch," Marco went on. "Hoopfest is only a week away, and we're woefully unprepared this year."

"Good plan. Are the boys competing in the youth division?"

"Yeah, it's Michael's last year at that level. He was trying to convince Sam Diaz to play instead of Oren, but Sam doesn't want to. Oren's ecstatic. It's the first year he's old enough."

Alex chuckled. Michael was the youngest of the Santoro cousins. He'd have lots of chances to play with the older boys. "I remember being the little kid no one wanted to have on their team. It's good for Michael."

"You think *you* had it bad?" Evan arched an eyebrow. "I'm four years younger than you, and I had to be twice as good before you'd let me play with you."

"You'll never be twice as good as me."

"In your dreams."

But all this wasn't solving the Marley problem. Alex lowered Lillian to Evan's arms. "Here, your turn." Then he turned to his dad. "Hey, I'm not sure if Marley is vegetarian. She's got a yard full of chickens, so I bet she doesn't eat poultry at least."

Dad's tongs halted over the grill. "Advance warning might have been nice."

"Yeah, well, *you* invited her, not me."

Dad chuckled, the sound echoed by the other men on the deck.

Alex pressed on. "And I'm not sure. She didn't say. All I know is she got mighty emotional when Eden captured half her birds and hauled them off, like they were her best friends in the whole world or something."

"Didn't Wesley and Kass take those hens?" asked Marco. "So all's well that ends well."

"Just saying I'm not sure she'll differentiate." Alex pointed at the marinated thighs, drumsticks, and breasts.

"Oh..."

Dad shook his head. "Your mother has lots of salads and side dishes. It will have to be good enough this time around. We'll see how it goes, and we can make adjustments for next time."

"Next time?" Alex raised his eyebrows at his father. "You figure you'll keep on inviting her for Sunday lunch?"

"Just helping you out this once, son. From here on, it's up to you."

Evan snickered, startling the baby into a whimper.

Alex should have known better than to bring up the subject. "Then this is one-time only, and it won't be a problem in the future."

"It always starts that way." Nathan took Lillian from Evan and cradled her close to his chest. "Shh, sweetheart. It's okay. Your mama and I are going to lock you up until you're thirty, so this isn't going to apply to you."

"Jas is only twenty-nine right now," Evan pointed out. "You going to talk like that, you should have left your wife in unmarried bliss for a while longer."

Nathan turned away, bouncing the infant. "Don't listen to Uncle Evan, baby girl. He doesn't know what he's talking about."

"So, you aren't going to put a move on Marley?" Evan elbowed Alex. "What are you waiting for, God to drop a voluptuous female in front of you with a wreath of flowers around her neck?"

Alex arched his brows. "Is that your idea of a dream woman? Seriously?" Though he could totally picture Marley with a lei. That'd be right up her alley. "In that case, it's a good thing your head will be stuck in textbooks for a couple of more years."

Dad laughed. "Would one of you grab me a platter from the kitchen and let your mother know we're ready out here?"

"I've got it." Alex pivoted toward the open patio door just in time to see Marley edging away from it.

Had she been listening? And, if she had, what exactly had she overheard?

arley should have known Alex's family would get ideas from her joining them for Sunday dinner. After all, his dad had positively gleamed when he invited her in the coffee shop. If only the first person to befriend her — if that's what she could call this relationship with Alex — wasn't a guy. A guy with a big family. A guy with a big Italian family that sprouted curiosity like wings and apparently had designs on finding the poor fellow a wife.

In that case, they'd be sorely disappointed with Marley. She wasn't getting married anytime soon, like ever. She'd seen too much in her twenty-four years. Her parents' repeated breakups. Her stepbrother treating women like objects and wondering why he was alone. Even Reverend Smith's wife had finally left him. Good for her getting out from under that man's thumb.

Pastor Tomas wasn't like Reverend Smith. For one thing, he smiled. Did that mean the people in his church were nicer and less judgmental, too? If the Santoros were a reasonable sample, then yes.

Marley only wanted friends. She didn't want marriage. She didn't even want a man who looked good holding a newborn, because the planet did not need more humans on it.

The patio door slid open and Alex appeared, his eyes snapping to meet her gaze. And, yeah, he'd looked good holding his niece. Not that she'd ever say so, or even think it again.

She offered him a tentative smile. "Hey."

"Hey. How are you doing? Did Jasmine abandon you already?"

"She needed to use the restroom."

"Ah." Alex took a few steps closer. "Dad sent me in for a platter."

And this was her problem how? By the look on his face, he expected something. But what?

"He's grilling chicken. Sorry about that."

She blinked. "Sorry?"

"Um, yeah? Because you probably don't eat chicken."

Understanding washed over her. "It's fine."

Alex frowned. "But...?" He drew the single word out.

"No, really. I don't eat a lot of meat, mostly because I can't afford it. But so long as we're not talking about my friends, it's okay."

He searched her face. The face that was getting warmer by the second. "If you're sure. There's likely lots of other food, too. You don't have to try everything."

Wasn't that sweet of him? "Thanks. But it's fine." In fact, the aromas drifting in through the patio doors had her mouth watering and her stomach gurgling.

"Alessandro!" Marietta called. "Is your papa nearly finished with the chicken?"

"Yes, Nonna." Alex looked toward his grandmother. "I've come for a platter. Then we can gather around the table." He gave Marley another quizzical glance then headed toward the kitchen.

Marietta must be pushing eighty if not more, but her eyes were sharp. So sharp they seemed to see into Marley's heart and soul. "Marley. What is that short for?"

"Um... it's just my name. It's not short for anything. And I'm also not named for anyone in particular." Not a dog, not a reggae singer, and not a Dickensian character.

The old woman frowned. "It's not a proper name."

Marley's spine stiffened of its own accord. "It's mine, and I like it."

"Nonna, leave her alone." Jasmine entered the family room. "You don't like my name, either, but you still like me. I think." She hooked her arm through Marley's and whispered conspiratorially, "Jasmine is not a particularly Italian name, after all."

"Humph."

"She tried to call me *Gelsomino* when I was a baby — that's the herb jasmine in Italian — but my dad made her stop. Whew, right? What a mouthful. And, for the record, Alex's full legal name is Alexander, not Alessandro."

Marietta glared at her granddaughter.

Marley managed to hold back the smirk that wanted out. She squeezed Jasmine's arm in appreciation.

"And you paint chickens?" the old lady went on. "Did you bring something to show?"

Should she have brought a painting as a hostess gift? It hadn't even crossed Marley's mind. Her family hadn't stood much on that kind of formality. If anything, they'd brought a six-pack of beer.

"Nonna..." Jasmine's voice warned.

"I was only asking," Marietta said with a huff.

"Oh!" Marley tugged her phone out of her skirt pocket and opened it to her Instagram account. She held the device to Marietta.

The woman took it, scowling, but her face relaxed as she studied the image. "So many hearts. You are famous?"

How many was 'so many?' Marley hadn't checked her account for a few days.

"Let me see." Jasmine leaned in and scrolled down. "I love these, Marley! So whimsical. So cheerful. No wonder you have thousands of followers. I'll be one more, for sure. Are you selling these somewhere?"

Marley's head reeled. "I will be. Kass at the bakery wants—"

"Oh, that's great! Bridgeview loves to support local artists and artisans, but Kass and Hailey get enough outside traffic to make a big difference, too. I bet you do well there."

"Thank you." What else was there to say? Marley glanced at Jasmine's grandmother, who'd taken over the scrolling, her face softening with each motion. Was she winning the old woman over one chicken at a time?

Not that it mattered. This wasn't her family, who'd only laughed at her lame attempts at art. She wasn't looking for anyone's confirmation beyond Instagram. Although, yes, a handful of paying fans would be good. She needed to face the likelihood that few would plunk down their hard-earned money on her silly hobby. When she dropped off the canvases on Monday, she'd ask about that job.

HUH. She'd taken a chicken thigh off the platter and even had a few bites of it.

Alex had figured she was only being polite. Maybe that was still the case. She was a strange mix of outgoing and shy, maybe even insecure. He'd never met anyone like her in Bridgeview, and she was rather fascinating.

Evan smirked at him across the table. Alex raised his eyebrows back, which caused his kid brother to cut his eyes toward Marley then back at Alex. Alex narrowed his gaze, and Evan laughed.

His baby brother could go dunk his head. *Fascinating* wasn't a code word for being interested in a romantic sense. He didn't even want to date anyone right now, remember? If he did, there were a few more suitable options, like Tina, Bridgeview's kindergarten teacher. She was pretty, pleasant, and a career-minded woman. But, no. With his thirtieth birthday still nearly three years away, it was too early to be watching out for Ms. Right.

Ms. Right was definitely not the gardening-challenged, chicken-loving artist sitting right next to him at his parents' dinner table. Not a chance.

Although she was cute in a hippie sort of way, which wasn't Alex's style at all.

He shouldn't be looking at her. Not with Evan snickering across the table until their entire family was sending speculative glances between the two of them.

Evan was so juvenile.

"Please pass the dinner rolls," said Daria.

Alex reached for the basket in front of his plate just as Marley did, and their fingers brushed. What on earth was that tingle all about? He pulled back. She could pass the rolls. Only she withdrew as well.

Evan guffawed.

Alex skewered him with a glare, not that it made any difference.

Marco chuckled.

Alex lifted the basket — alone, this time — and passed it to his dad. Man. Even Dad was grinning. Did his entire family consist of twelve-year-olds? Seemed like it.

Beside him, Marley picked up her grilled chicken and dug into it.

He should never have presumed to smooth the way for her. It had only given the testosterone-driven side of his family something to speculate about. But would he have gotten off any easier if he hadn't tried? Not when Dad had issued the dinner invitation. For a minute there, Alex had panicked that his uncles would insert themselves, too, just for the front-row seats.

There were no front-row seats. There was no show, regardless of what anyone thought. Dad had put Alex in this awkward position, and Nonna always had dinner at Uncle Franco's on the third Sunday of the month. Yet, here she was, as curious as the rest of them.

Alex had half a mind to get to his feet, set his family straight, and head up the hill to his own house. He'd never do it, of course. Not only would it be insulting to Marley, it would be rude to his elders. But the temptation was strong.

"May I have some more of that Caprese salad?" he asked.

Nathan passed the serving dish of tomatoes, mozzarella, and basil to Jasmine, who passed it to Marley, who passed it to Alex.

"Want a bit more?" He held the dish toward her.

"No, thank you. It was very good, though."

She'd barely eaten a thing. Was it because the flavors were strange to her, or was it nerves? Or maybe she didn't usually have a hefty appetite. Alex spent too much time around guys with hollow legs. Guys who could pack away four times what she'd put on her plate and be back in half an hour looking for more.

"Save room for dessert," Mom admonished. "Daria brought a lovely coffee cake."

"Mmm, sounds good." Alex forked some of the Caprese to his plate. "There's always room for dessert."

"I don't like coffee," grumbled Arie.

Marco ruffled his youngest son's hair. "It doesn't have coffee in it, buddy. It's called that because it tastes good *with* coffee."

"That's weird."

Caden leaned around his dad to look at his little brother. "I'll have your piece. It has cinnamon and sugar and nuts on top. You won't like it."

"I will, too, if there's no coffee."

Chuckles rounded the table, and Alex relaxed. Yay for his nephews stealing the attention away from him and Marley.

There was no him and Marley.

But there could be. Maybe.

He didn't want there to be. That corner office wasn't in the bag. He didn't have time for a relationship. If he did, it wouldn't be with her.

Keep telling yourself that, buddy.

Great, now even his inner self thought Marley might be a good idea. She wasn't. Not by a long shot.

Marley giggled at something Jasmine had said too low for Alex to catch. It was a pleasant sound.

He glanced her way, making sure to keep the peek too quick for Evan to pounce on. Her long curls veiled her face. He could reach over and tuck the strands behind her ear—

Was he absolutely crazy? Obviously.

Alex took a stab at a tomato slice on his plate then polished off the salad and the last piece of chicken on his plate. "Great meal, Mom. Thank you." He leaned to peer at Jasmine. Incidentally, she was beyond Marley. "There was nothing herbal besides the basil and Mom's traditional marinade, so I assume you had no hand in this meal. You still milking that just-had-a-baby thing for whatever it's worth?"

Jasmine rolled her eyes. "Try to convince me you don't like the salads I usually bring. And Mom wouldn't let me. I think I'll be allowed to cook again by the Fourth of July." She looked at Marley. "You should come to the fireworks with us. Have you seen them at Riverside Park before? Spokane does them up right."

Who was this *us* his sister meant?

"I haven't been to the Fourth here, no. That sounds fun." Marley shot a quick glance at Alex.

"Sure," he said easily. "There's always a huge contingent of Bridgeview folks meeting up there. You might as well join us." That didn't sound too much like a date invitation, did it? Because it wasn't one. Not even close. Just him going along with his sister, because lifelong experience had taught him the simplest route to peace.

He'd save his rebellion for when it really mattered. He wouldn't waste it on arguing about something he kind of wanted to do anyway. And, no, he wasn't going to examine that thought beyond not wanting anyone he knew to be so alone they depended on chickens to be their best friends.

Jasmine was only being altruistic. For once, his sister was right. He could endorse that.

Marley offered him a fleeting smile before turning back to Jasmine. "Thank you. That's very thoughtful."

Jasmine flicked her eyebrows at Alex. "I've been dying to meet my brother's new... neighbor. Lillian and I will pop over to see you one day soon for a visit. Maybe you'll show me more of your art?"

Great. Alex could read between the lines. What his sister really meant was she'd tell Marley all about *him*. If this was how it felt to be on the Santoro hot seat, he could live without it. He sent a silent apology to Jasmine and Peter and Rob and anyone else in his family he'd teased and badgered early in a new relationship.

It was different, though. He and Marley weren't together. They wouldn't ever be. Why did that thought feel so deflating?

Best not to dwell on it.

9

*M*arley tugged the bistro's door open in mid-afternoon and grinned as voices and laughter poured out from many of the tables. One employee worked the coffee machine while another prepped a sandwich. Several customers chatted while they waited. Kass, the owner, was nowhere in sight.

It seemed rude to budge in line to ask for Kass without buying anything, though Marley hated to add to the lineup. She clutched her expandable case, bulging with a dozen paintings, and shifted from one foot to the other until it was her turn.

"Hi! What can I get for you?" The cashier smiled at Marley. She looked tired, tendrils of dark hair escaping her bun.

"A cup of chamomile tea, please? And is Kass in? She asked me to come by and talk to her."

"Sure, I'll call her. Are you Marley, by any chance? I'm Ava Santoro."

Another Santoro? But this one wasn't Alex's sister, at

least. She'd already met the one and only. "Yes, I'm Marley. Pleased to meet you."

"You've met my brother Peter. He lives next door to you. With our cousin Alex." The young woman's blue eyes sparkled with something Marley didn't wish to speculate about.

"Thanks for clarifying. There seem to be a lot of your relatives in this neighborhood."

Ava chuckled. "You have no idea. Although, I believe you've met our nonna, Marietta."

Marley let out a long breath. The elderly woman's piercing gaze had haunted her since Sunday. Oh, she'd been polite enough after pushing Marley about her name. But the way she'd studied Marley had been plenty unnerving. "I have."

"She's something else, huh? She thinks she's the queen of Bridgeview."

"Ava, if you can't say anything nice about Nonna, don't say anything at all." The other girl, younger by several years, set a tall mug of coffee on the pickup counter for the middle-aged man who'd been ahead of Marley. Then she turned with a smile. "Hi, I'm Gabriella. Another Santoro cousin. You're right. There are tons of us around here, but our nonna doesn't bite. She just wants the best for all of us grandkids."

Ava rolled her eyes. "And she's sure she knows what that is. All I'm telling Marley is, she shouldn't let Nonna bully her into liking — or *not* liking — Alex."

What? A flush shot up Marley's face. Why had Ava said that so loudly? Who all might have overheard? "She's got nothing to worry about there."

Gabriella nudged Ava. "Why not? I'd guess Alex is a

pretty good catch. Although he's kind of serious, if you like that type."

Marley shifted the portfolio to her other hand. "I, um..."

"Go get Kass, Gabby. I'll prep Marley's tea. We can talk about Alex later." Ava smirked at Marley. "Or not, as the case might be. Grab a seat, and I'll bring out your tea."

Oh, man. Marley dug into her wallet, her face flushed and her gaze averted. She wanted friends. Needed friends, but why did everyone think a woman her age was looking for a man? She wasn't. Not at all. And if she were, it wouldn't be someone like her next-door neighbor.

She settled into the same chair she'd sat in last week and began stacking her paintings on the table, but her thoughts refused to come along. Instead... what *would* her dream guy be like? Would he be more like her, ragtag with a broken past and no post-secondary education? If she were fantasizing already, she might as well dream bigger. Better. A cute guy with a solid work ethic, a good job, and a close extended family.

A guy like Alex Santoro.

Yeah, no. He was her polar opposite. But might that not be a good thing? Because heaven help the household where there were two adults as flaky as she was.

Not like she had anything to say about it. Alex was no more interested in her than she was in him. He'd only been a gentleman in touching her lower back. He hadn't felt a thing when their hands brushed over that basket of rolls. Sure, his family seemed intent on teasing him, but that was all about their expectations, not about her.

Kass set two cups of tea on the table and lowered herself onto the turquoise chair across from Marley. She leaned back and closed her eyes for a moment.

Marley studied her lined face. "Are you okay?"

"Not really." Kass offered a wan smile. "I'm on my feet way too many hours, and I've started having some early labor pains. My obstetrician commanded me to quit working, but I can't. We might have to shorten business hours so the staff can keep up once the baby's here. Nine months ago, I was positive we had plenty of time to hire the right person to fill in, but the bistro has only gotten busier."

"You kind of offered me a job last week."

Kass focused in on Marley's eyes. "I'll offer it again, if it helps. Our biggest need is to cover the lunch rush through to closing. Eleven to five. Now that school's out for the summer, Gabriella agreed to a split shift, though I hate to do that to anyone."

"Eleven to five?" Marley was an early riser. She could get a lot of gardening and painting done before ten-thirty. "I've worked in a café before, but it was a lot different than this."

"We'll train you, if you're serious? I can't begin to tell you what a godsend you would be."

Marley didn't need to hear the words. She could see the hope and relief flooding Kass's face. "Sure. I could do that for the summer, at least. We could reconsider when you're ready to come back."

Kass threw up her hands. "Thank You, Jesus."

That was... weird. Though Marley had seen the redhead down the side of the church on Sunday morning with her husband and their son. She didn't think she'd ever had anyone thank God for her before, though. It was a nice change from being cursed and yelled at.

"When can you start? Today? Tomorrow?"

Marley chuckled. "You could show me around today, if

you like, but it's already way past eleven. Will I need a uniform or anything?"

"White top with sleeves. Black pants or shorts or skirt, not much above the knee. The turquoise aprons complete the outfit."

She could make a quick trip to a thrift store this afternoon. City transit came through often enough.

"Let me enter your paintings into inventory and get that out of the way first. I've got your paperwork right here." Kass attached coded stickers to the back of each canvas while Marley recorded the numbers. "Did you meet Ava? I'll have her give you a tour. You'll be working with her a lot, though she gets off an hour earlier than you will." Kass smiled at Marley. "I can't tell you how much I appreciate you helping a pregnant woman out. It's a huge relief."

Marley felt the same way. The chickens provided abundant artistic inspiration, but they weren't so great at conversation.

ALEX TROOPED into Bridgeview Bakery and Bistro Saturday afternoon in high spirits with his brothers and cousin. Hoopfest weekend was always such a buzz.

"Hey!" yelled Gabriella. "How'd you guys do?"

Peter pointed both thumbs to the floor. "The Bulldogs are out, but we put up a good fight."

"Win, lose, win," Evan clarified. "Better than a year ago when Peter broke his ankle the week before." He elbowed Peter.

"Dominic needed a chance last year to show how out of shape he was," Peter said good-naturedly.

Gabriella's older brother, Dominic, was in med school in Seattle. And, yeah, it had showed he hadn't been playing much three-on-three for a few years, let alone with his Santoro cousins. Alex hated to think the Bulldogs' glory days were behind them, but with Basil gone, they just didn't have as good a showing as they used to when they were younger and more eager. Evan might talk a good game, but he wasn't as agile as Basil. Times like this, Alex missed his older brother. Most of the rest of the time, he didn't. Not really.

"I'll get you guys some pop. What else would you like?"

Man, he was starving. "Cinnamon roll over here."

"Me, too," echoed Peter. The others nodded.

Gabriella laughed. "Four cinnamon rolls, coming right up." She turned to the worker beside her. "Would you plate those while I get the drinks?"

Alex's heart stilled. He hadn't even noticed Marley there. She looked a lot different wearing the bistro uniform and with her long curls braided back. He grinned. "Hey, Marley."

She flashed him a quick smile. "Hi. Sure, I'll get the rolls."

Marco, Peter, and Evan edged toward the pickup end of the counter, Evan hitting replay on the last two minutes of their final game. It had been so close.

"How long have you been working here?" Alex asked. Now that he was closer, he could see Marley still wore a bohemian-style skirt, only this one was all black. He managed to hold in his grin.

"Since Wednesday." Her hand trembled as she lifted a cinnamon roll out with a pair of tongs.

"Cool." Had he seen her around the yard less the last

few days? He'd spent most of his spare time practicing basketball over by the community center, so he hadn't popped by the bistro after work, either. "I've been kind of busy this week."

She scanned his red Bulldogs tank and snagged another cinnamon roll. "Some sort of sporting event?"

"Only the biggest and greatest three-on-three competition in the world."

"What is that?"

How could she live in Spokane and not know? Right. She was new here. "Basketball with three guys on the court at a time from each team. There's four of us so we can rotate in and out."

Her eyebrows lifted as she set the third plate on the counter. "Just guys?"

"There are all female, all male, and co-ed divisions. Our team just happens to be all guys."

"Hmm."

"Do you play basketball?" He vaguely remembered pointing out the court under the bridge to her back a couple of weeks ago. She hadn't seemed interested.

"No. I'm not very athletic." She straightened the plates and offered a fleeting smile. "I think I'm supposed to carry these out to your table."

"Let me grab two."

Marley followed him toward the end table where the Bulldogs had gathered, along with a couple of other Spokane teams who'd also faced early elimination. She passed her plates to Marco and Peter then flashed Alex a quick smile. "Thanks."

He watched her walk away.

"Dude. That my roll?" Evan grabbed one of the plates

Alex had carried. "Quit drooling over the cute waitress and get in here."

Drooling? "As if." He elbowed his kid brother and pulled a chair at an angle before straddling it, listening to the tournament rehash. Sue him if that angle allowed him to keep a surreptitious eye on Marley as she served the next group to enter the bistro. With any luck, Evan wouldn't notice.

Marley glanced over, though. Her gaze shifted away as a flush crept up her cheeks.

Huh. He'd never had that effect on a woman before. At least, not that he knew of. Or maybe it was the effect she had on him that made him notice.

Alex wasn't looking for a girlfriend, remember? But... why not? Lots of guys his age were married. Some even had a child or two. Marco'd had three. That whole being thirty with the corner office thing was something Alex had made up himself. Something his boss had fed into. Yeah, he'd asserted it to his family a time or two, but it wasn't a rule or anything. He could change it if he wanted to.

He could invite Marley on a date.

Last time he'd asked someone out, he'd asked her to marry him and been shot down. Poor Linnea. He'd been such a dunce, trying to save her from her problems. Save her from Logan. Things had been awkward for a while after that. It didn't help that Jasmine had made sure he knew how dumb he'd been. Thankfully, Linnea and Logan hadn't held it against Alex for long. They were his good friends now. His tenants, even.

Was he only interested in Marley because she reminded him of Linnea? Someone with a rough background who needed a gallant knight on a black steed to swoop in and save her? There was definitely that aspect, but it wasn't the only thing.

Was it?

Alex needed to think about that a bit more before getting in over his head. Even praying about it would not go amiss. He'd never prayed about a girl before, at least not beyond asking God to bring the right one around... eventually.

Was now later?

An elbow jabbed his side, and a slosh of ginger ale landed on his red shorts. "Hey!"

Evan grinned at him from beneath raised eyebrows. "Dude, you're totally spaced. Tomlinson asked you a question."

Alex focused on the player across the table. "Yeah? What's up?"

A dozen guys hooted with laughter.

Great.

10

*T*he bistro was closed Sundays and Mondays, which made church attendance an easy decision. It was a nice change to wear something brightly colored and keep her hair down, too.

Bridgeview Bible Church didn't seem quite as intimidating as it had the week before. Marley had barely stepped inside the bright foyer when Ava swooped in from the other side.

"Marley! Won't you sit with me?"

"Thanks. That would be great." Except her coworker dragged her up to the fourth pew from the front. So much for hiding. Still, it was nice to have a friend near her own age, even though Ava had graduated from college this spring with a teaching degree, and Marley had never given college more than a wistful thought. She'd barely survived high school in one piece.

She stood when everyone around her did and listened to them sing worship songs to God while she read the words on the screen up front. Words about God being greater, stronger, and higher than any other. Around her, hands lifted in praise. Peaceful faces with eyes closed tipped up as though they had nothing to fear.

Marley liked the God proclaimed here, but was He the real one? Had Reverend Smith known a different one? Oh, there seemed to be similarities, for sure. But as Pastor Tomas expounded on 'God is wise,' she found herself realizing that just as stubbornness seemed negative while perseverance seemed positive, many of the things she'd been taught about God could be seen from different angles. Huh.

A man she'd seen coming and going from Alex's house next door slid onto the piano bench at the close of the sermon and leaned into his microphone. "This song is taken from First Timothy 1:17. Please join me."

She listened to the words of praise to the only wise God. By the second time around, she joined in, hesitantly, quietly, and felt a lift to her spirit. She could trust this God and give Him honor and glory. He seemed like a good King, one who used His powers for love not punishment.

Was Reverend Smith wrong about punishment, too? Marley shifted uneasily in her seat. God knew she wasn't perfect. She'd tried, but she'd messed up time and again. She'd never been enough for anyone. How could she be enough for God?

ALEX HAD SAT in the row behind Marley with a good view of the side of her face as Pastor Tomas preached. She looked hungry. Yearning. What did that mean of her faith? How could he even dream of getting to know her better if she didn't believe? Yet, how could she look so wistful if the Holy Spirit wasn't working in her heart?

He couldn't pursue her. He remembered the struggle Kass had gone through when she'd fallen in love with Wesley before he believed. How she'd stepped away from their fledgling relationship and just prayed for him. God had answered that prayer. Two years later, there was no doubt Wesley's faith was real and active.

Alex's gaze drifted across the sanctuary to where Kass, Wesley, and Sebastian always sat, but the space was empty. He frowned slightly. They never missed unless they were out of town, and surely, they wouldn't go away with Kass so close to her due date.

Was she in labor? Alex felt like a pro on the topic with his sister having gone through all this just a few weeks ago with Lillian's birth.

The benediction barely pronounced, Alex excused himself past the others in his pew until he found Kass's cousin and business partner, Hailey. "Hey, is Kass okay?"

Hailey's startled gaze latched onto his. "Yes? Why not?"

"She's not here."

Hailey laughed just as her phone buzzed. She glanced down then zeroed back on Alex. "How did you know?" She tilted the screen at Alex, but it went blank before he could read the entire message.

Taking Kass to hospital...

Must have been from Wesley. "Lucky guess?"

She swiped the screen open and read the rest. "Astrid is on her way to pick up Sebastian. Kass's contractions are twelve minutes apart. I need to get over there." Hailey grabbed her purse and rose before sinking back onto the padded pew. "I guess she doesn't need me. She has Wesley."

Alex crooked a grin at her. "As a guy with a pile of cousins, I'm guessing she'll always need you. You two only have each other, right? It's just a little different now."

"Yeah, there's only the two of us. Growing up here in Santoro Land, I've seen what a big clan can be like." She chuckled and looked away. "Pros and cons, I imagine."

She was likely thinking of Basil, who'd made a big fuss about how his relatives stifled him even before his drunk driving conviction. "Mostly pros, regardless of what my brother says." Alex watched Hailey's reaction.

Yup. Her eyes flicked to his then away as a bit of color infused her cheeks.

"Basil's an idiot."

Hailey pulled to her feet. "Yep. Seems to be. I really should go now."

Hmm. Was she dodging talk of Basil, or only concerned for Kass? "Don't worry too much."

"Easy for you to say." She leaned forward and tapped Eden's shoulder. "Kass is in labor."

Alex knew when he wasn't wanted. While he'd been talking to Hailey, pews around them emptied as folks angled toward the foyer. He'd be headed to his parents' house for Sunday dinner in a few minutes, but it wouldn't be the same as last week. Marley had increased his awareness of everything around him, and today would seem a little dull — less vibrant — without her there. Unless Mom or Dad had gone and invited her again without consulting him?

His gaze narrowed on Marley walking with Ava as they disappeared out the door, heads together. Marley's long reddish curls contrasted sharply with Ava's deep brown.

He didn't need to worry about Marley. She worked with

Ava, and they'd obviously hit it off. That was good, right? She had a friend. She didn't need him.

Alex scoffed lightly. Like she ever *had* needed him. Did he have some sort of savior complex, thinking he was the only person who could solve problems? He shook his head. Too often it was true. He saw situations and solutions quickly and clearly, and it was hard to pull back when the fix was on someone else.

A clout on the shoulder brought him back to reality. "Dude, you talking to yourself again?"

Evan. Of course, Evan. "Not at all. You must be confusing me with your own loud thoughts."

His brother's gaze flicked to the door then back at Alex. "You lose your girlfriend?"

"I don't have a girlfriend. As you know." Alex glared at his little brother. "Grow up."

"Oh, right. It's only in your dreams."

"Again, you're mistaking my dreams for yours. You want a girlfriend? Ask Marley out." He wished he could claw those words out of the air before they reached Evan's ears, but by the smirk on his brother's face, he'd heard, all right.

"I just might. She's about my age, don't you think?"

"No idea." One of many conversations Alex had *not* had with Marley. But why had he given Evan approval to date her? Not that his brother required anyone's permission.

Evan leaned close. "It could be fun to see you glowering with jealousy. Might light a fire under your own backside."

Alex locked eyes with him. "If you've got anything but pure motives for dating, skip it. She's not a pawn in your stupid childish games."

A chuckle wafted over Evan's shoulder as he sauntered away.

Great. All the peace and joy he'd experienced at the end of the service had just dissipated.

***

DID everyone in Bridgeview have family dinners on Sunday after church, or was it just the Santoros? Marley followed Ava in the door at her parents' house, still feeling a little awkward. Ava's dad, Dino, was one of the uncles who'd eagerly watched when Ray invited her to dinner last week. He'd flashed a big grin when Ava told him and his wife, Betta, that Marley would be joining them today.

Ava scooped up a toddler as she entered the house and spun him around. "My nephew, Gavin," she said to Marley. "A little boy who needs all. The. Raspberries." With each pause, she blew spurts of bubbles on the little guy's neck.

He giggled and squirmed then gave Marley a shy smile as he nestled against Ava's shoulder.

"Come on through to the kitchen. Dad and Peter have a baseball game on TV."

"Ball." Gavin wiggled and kicked to get down.

Ava laughed as she set him on the floor. "They start 'em early around here. Come on. Have you met Peter's fiancée, Sadie, yet? Or my sister Dafne?"

"Sadie's my neighbor."

"Right." Ava led the way into a large, gleaming kitchen. "Marley, meet Dafne. Daf, this is Marley. She lives next door to Peter and started working at the bistro this week."

A girl in her late teens smiled and said hello before peering past her. "Where's Gav?"

"Watching the ball game with Dad and *Unca Petuh*."

"Okay."

Wait. This young girl was the toddler's mother? There was a story in there somewhere. She couldn't possibly be married. She didn't look old enough to be out of high school.

"Hi, Marley!" Sadie smiled at her from across the island. "I'm glad to hang out with you today."

"Thanks." Marley smiled back.

"How are your chickens doing?" Sadie went on. "If you ever have more eggs than you know what to do with, I'd love to buy some from you. I go through a lot of eggs."

"I do have a couple of dozen extra right now. Come on over later."

Sadie's face brightened. "Really? That's awesome."

"Drat." Ava sighed. "I was going to ask. Brittany is on an egg kick and we keep running out." She turned to Marley. "Britt is Gabby's older sister, so... another of my cousins. We have an apartment together over in Bridgeview Manor. You know that gorgeous brick building on Clarke?"

"I've seen it. It looks lovely."

"Yeah. It's got character. As does Brittany."

Sadie laughed. "There are a lot of Santoros around here, Marley, and half the neighborhood with a different surname are still related. That took some serious getting used to when I moved in last year."

"And most of us are outgoing." Dafne batted her lashes at Sadie. "Are we growing on you yet?"

"You know it."

"If you can't beat 'em, join 'em," Ava said with a laugh as she turned back to Marley, jiggling her eyebrows. "Sometimes offense is the best defense."

Um, what was she saying?

"Ooh!" Dafne's eyes sparkled. "I heard a rumor about you and Alex."

"Don't believe everything you hear." Sadie put up a cautionary hand. "Unless it happens to be true."

Best to feign nonchalance. "I'm not sure what you've heard, but there's no *me and Alex*." She air-quoted the words. "He's my next-door neighbor, but we don't know each other that well." Not saying there wasn't a part of her that would say yes to a bit more exposure to him, but how could anyone function in this neighborhood when entire clans speculated?

The back door opened, and Ava's mom and grand-mother entered. Marietta's shrewd eyes focused right on Marley's. "Marley. Good to see you again. Have you sold some of those chickens?"

Marley stared for a second. Her hens were so not for sale! Oh. Wait. The paintings. "One, so far." It had happened her second day at work. Kind of exciting, although Kass had handled the transaction.

"That is good. Will you make more?"

"Yes. I already have. I only work a six-hour shift, so I still have plenty of time to paint and garden." And hang out with Chloe, Deirdre, Gloria, Zephyr, and Bella, who were eager to spend time with her whenever she was outside. Sometimes Deirdre even snuck into the house.

"Good, good." The old woman nodded.

At least someone approved of her and her work ethic. Marley had the feeling that Marietta could be a harsh judge if she didn't.

"Okay, girls. Let's get lunch on the table." Betta turned to the slow cooker on the counter. "I wasn't expecting company today — it's fine, Marley. Don't worry about it.

You're welcome here. It's only that I would have made something fancier had I known. It's just stew and biscuits."

Ava leaned closer and whispered, "It's not even you she's apologizing to. It's Nonna. Nonna's Sunday schedule is a mess because she's following you around."

Marley pulled her friend aside. "Are you serious?"

"Yeah. She overhead me telling Mom I was inviting you and told Uncle Franco he could wait until next week."

"That's crazy. Why is she so interested in me?"

"Because she wants to make sure you're good enough for Alex."

"But..."

Ava winked. "I think you're winning her over."

"But... why? We're not a couple. He was only being polite because his dad—"

"You keep telling yourself that. Now, come on. I should warn you that Mom's biscuits are low-carb since Sadie came into our life. She's been on this massive diet for over a year and lost a boatload of weight." She shrugged. "The biscuits aren't bad, really. And Mom's learned to bake without sugar. You know how Astrid is always going on about the evils of sugar and processed flour at work? Well, she's taught Mom a few tricks so she can make stuff for Sadie."

"That's sweet." Or not, because what was dessert without sugar? But it did prove that the Santoro women would go out of their way to support the women their sons loved.

Would Alex's mom, too? Alex had been so concerned about the grilled chicken that Marley had to believe a word in advance would have seen a different protein source on the table last week.

Now if she could only figure out how to navigate this

complicated family without getting in too deep. Nice, surface friendships were best. That way people wouldn't figure out all her insecurities too quickly.

Dafne turned to Marley. "What did you think of Pastor Tomas's sermon this morning?"

So much for superficial.

11

*A*lex!"

He turned in the crowd. That had been his cousin Tony, hadn't it? He rarely saw the guy even though he'd moved back to Bridgeview last fall. With the opening of his restaurant, Antonio's, back in May, Tony rarely had time to socialize.

Alex clouted his cousin on the shoulder. "Hey! Good to see you. Did you close early tonight?"

"Yeah. Everyone in Spokane is right here in Riverside Park for the fireworks, so we decided to shut 'er down." Tony twisted his neck with a cracking sound. "Besides, I couldn't find any staff willing to work."

"I bet." Alex chuckled then lowered his voice. "I'm glad to see you, dude. Sometimes I feel like the odd man out with so many cousins married or engaged. I'm here with Peter and Sadie."

"I hear you. We can buddy up tonight." Tony fell into step beside him, and they followed in the direction the couple had gone. "Although I'm not sure why you're not dating. You're established in your career and have your own place. Where I'm fighting the biggest learning curve of my life and living in Nonna's basement."

"But you've wanted to start your own restaurant since you were in high school."

"Yeah." Tony shrugged. "But it's still a ton of work. I have to laugh at all the uncles thinking I needed to live with Nonna so she wouldn't be alone. I see her about twice a week for half an hour. Sometimes I envy you just working for the man, you know? You work, what, eight to four, five days a week? And then you're done and don't have to think about the office anymore."

"True, there are advantages. But I've got other goals to reach before I get serious about anyone." Alex pointed toward the mown area where Peter set up two lawn chairs. He hadn't felt like hauling a chair this far. He'd just sit on the grass. "Over there."

Tony's elbow caught his ribs. "The corner office? Who cares, anyway? You're making good money. Relax. Be happy."

If anyone epitomized relaxing and being happy, it seemed to be Marley Montgomery. She lived in the moment in a rundown house with an overgrown yard working a part-time, minimum-wage job, but she seemed contented. Alex had seen her out in her yard last night, arms outspread, eyes closed, twirling as the setting sun caught her curls. Her chickens had gathered around her amid green shoots poking up from her small cultivated garden patch.

He'd sidled back in the door before she'd noticed him, but he couldn't help thinking how satisfied, how peaceful, she looked.

"Hey, Peter. Sadie," came Tony's voice.

Alex blinked back to Riverside Park. Beside the couple, Ava spread an old quilt with the help of Dafne and... Marley? He'd thought she might come with Jasmine and Nathan. He'd forgotten she was friends with Ava, since they worked together. Ava was a good kid, and she'd kick his shins for thinking of her like that. She was only two years younger than Alex, but she'd always been the tagalong to the gang of older boys.

So had he, of course, but that hadn't made him Ava's ally. Even then, he'd been reaching forward, thinking big. Was that so wrong? A man needed to have goals. Needed to strive toward them. No one would do it for him.

Marley giggled at something Dafne said as she settled onto the ratty quilt that looked like one Nonna had made for her grandkids a dozen years ago. His was pristine, folded on a shelf in his closet with paper between the folds. Google had said that would preserve it best.

"Alex?"

Peter's knowing grin caught him as he turned slightly. "You look lost in thought."

Alex shook his head slowly. He'd probably been staring at Marley. Hopefully, he'd been staring at the quilt instead. "Is this the quilt Nonna made for you?" he asked Ava. That might get Peter off his back.

Maybe.

"Yes!" Ava gracefully lowered herself between Marley and Dafne like the dancer she was. "I just love this thing and use it every chance I get. I'm not as fond of the colors as when I was twelve, but it's still like a hug from Nonna every time I use it."

A hug from Nonna?

Peter poked the back of Alex's knees, nearly buckling him. "Dude. Sit down. You're blocking my view."

All right, then. He'd been told. He settled on the edge of the quilt. He couldn't help that Marley sat on this side, could he?

Sadie giggled.

Which meant Peter had been gossiping about him. It would be too embarrassing to call him out here. Thankfully the sun had set and the evening shadows stretched long. With any luck, they were long enough to hide the warmth on his cheeks.

Again, though, why worry what people thought? They all told him to get a life, anyway, and Marley was kind of interesting. More than interesting. He glanced sideways as he drew his knees toward his chest.

She had done the same thing, her long skirt tucked around her legs.

Had he ever seen her in jeans? In shorts? He couldn't remember if he had. See? She was strange. He shouldn't think thoughts about her. Any kind of thoughts.

Until she flashed a smile toward him. "Hi, Alex."

A gentleman would have spoken first. Would have asked if it were okay for him to sit there. Dad had taught him better than this. "Hi, Marley. I should have asked if you were saving this spot for someone else."

"No, it's fine."

"Thanks." He didn't dare look at her too long. Instead he leaned forward until Dafne was in his line of sight. "I don't see Gavin. How's he doing?"

"Mom said she'd keep him tonight so I could get out for a few hours. The noise of the fireworks freaks him out."

Alex nodded. "I can see that. It does get rather loud."

"They scared me when I was little, too," Marley put in. "I liked watching them on TV with the sound off, but not in person." A pensive frown crossed her face.

"Bad experience?" He leaned a little closer, until his arm touched her shoulder with a gentle pressure.

She took a deep breath and let it go before flashing him a quick smile. "You could say that." She shifted away.

The spot on his arm suddenly felt cool with the contract broken. Which was ridiculous, since it had only lasted a few seconds. But a sudden vision of a scared curly-haired little girl made him want to wrap his arm around her shoulders.

Whoa, Alex. Down, boy.

Yeah, he definitely didn't know her well enough to offer comfort. But... he could change that. Tony was right. Alex didn't really need to wait until he was thirty to start dating. That had been a silly, self-preserving decision he'd made after Linnea.

He looked at Marley. Would she be willing to get to know him? He studied her profile in the dusky light. Her tossed-back curls, her upturned nose, her slightly parted lips. The lips had had distracted him since they'd first met nearly a month ago.

He'd only kissed once. Linnea. He'd been so desperate to prove he could be what she needed. Thankfully, she'd known that wasn't true... and that kiss should have told him. It had been a total non-starter, though heaven knew he'd tried to start something with it.

What a dummy he'd been. In a nutshell, fear of being rejected all over again had kept his gaze focused on anything but women. His high-powered job. His house. Three-on-three.

He'd had a front row seat to a few relationships playing

out over those years. Linnea's with Logan, for instance. Jasmine and Nathan. Peter and Sadie. Not one of them had gone from casual liking to engaged without a hiccup. They'd weathered storms that drew them closer together and strengthened them.

Could he stick his neck out there again and risk rejection?

The first rocket shot in the air with an explosion he felt to his bones, and red, white, and blue flared into the sky.

Beside him, Marley winced.

Alex straightened his legs and braced his arms on the quilt. So what if that meant one arm angled behind Marley, brushing against her just enough that the hair on it leaned toward her. What would she do with that almost-touch?

She glanced his way, and their gazes held as two more rockets lit the night sky.

Maybe she was interested. Maybe he could take a chance. Baby steps, and all that.

IT WAS all Marley could do not to lean back just a smidge and really feel the pressure of Alex's arm against her back. As it was, she felt strangely secure even with fireworks shooting above her... and inside her.

But they were surrounded by a bunch of his cousins. No way in the world had at least one of them *not* noticed his position. That long look telling her his arm meant something would convey the same thing to any of them.

Marley tingled inside and out, but she stared up at the dark sky, barely seeing the fireworks, barely even hearing them. The popping bursts went on and on while every kind of pyrotechnics she'd ever heard of shot up then showered down in glistening color.

She felt the tension change in his arm as he leaned over. "Enjoying the fireworks?"

Alex was so close, angling in, his eyes lit by the latest rocket, his lips curved in a smile.

"Yes..." she breathed.

Did he know she meant both kinds? He must, because his smile teased upward even as he shifted just a hair closer to close the tiny gap there'd been between his arm and her back.

What did a hot guy like him see in her? She was an invisible nobody who happened to live next door. If only she hadn't tossed her chickens over the fence that day and attracted his notice. But what if she hadn't? Would he still be smiling at her in these flashes of light on the Fourth of July?

And why be attracted to him? Sure, he was all kinds of cute, but so were many other men. Alex had that huge family and a meddling grandmother, which should be enough to scare Marley off. But it was strangely inviting at the same time.

He leaned a little closer, his breath warm on her face.

Marley froze. No way was he going to kiss her. Not here. Not now.

"Could I interest you in a date on Saturday night?" he whispered.

She forced herself to relax a hair. Of course he wasn't going to steal a smooch. He wasn't that kind of man. But a date? Really? She searched his pleading eyes. He seemed to be holding his breath, worried she'd say no. "Sounds... fun."

"Really?"

How could he doubt her interest? She pressed a little more against his arm, feeling the solid muscles. For a guy with an office job, he had quite a few. "Sure."

"I'll get your phone number later so we can make a plan and keep in touch."

"Okay."

A staccato of pops startled her, but his arm provided a firm anchor as the light show crescendoed to a close. When the park lights began to brighten, Marley shifted away from him.

Ava turned to her. "Told you Spokane had great fireworks. What did you think?"

"You were right. They're the best I've ever seen." Was that only because they amplified the sparks between her and Alex? Not only, but that extra level of awareness sure helped.

Dafne jumped to her feet and stretched. "We'd better get going before someone trips over us."

On the other side, Peter folded his lawn chair. The other guy, whom she hadn't met yet, reached over and punched Alex's shoulder. "Ready, cuz?"

Of course. Another relative. It was obvious from the dark curly hair and classic good looks.

Alex rose to his feet then reached for her hand and pulled her upright.

Oh! She blinked. What had just happened?

"Tony, I'd like you to meet Marley Montgomery, my next-door neighbor. Marley, my cousin Tony. You may have seen that new restaurant between Bridgeview and downtown. Antonio's? That's his brainchild."

Tony grinned and reached to shake her hand. The hand that had still been tucked in Alex's.

She disentangled it and accepted Tony's greeting. "Nice to meet you. The building with the porticos out front?"

"That's the one." Tony's gaze shifted between her and Alex. "You guys should come for dinner sometime."

Alex's fingers tangled with hers, his focus still on his cousin. "How about Saturday? Reserve us a table for, say, seven?"

Tony's eyes danced as the park lights illuminated the area. "Sounds good." He jabbed Alex's shoulder again and turned to Ava. "Hey, can I give you a hand with that quilt?"

Hand-in-hand, Peter and Sadie disappeared into the crowd as Tony folded the quilt, chatting with the girls.

Marley allowed Alex to guide her away from his cousins, though she'd caught a ride down with Ava and shouldn't desert her.

Finally Alex found a less crowded spot and turned to Marley, catching her other hand as well. "Sorry if I put you on the spot there. But I really do want to take you out and get to know you, and I was already thinking of Antonio's."

"It's fine. I like Italian food." And, apparently, Italian men. At least one in particular.

12

*P*eter held up both hands. "It's cool, Alex. Really. But remember that going to church doesn't make someone a Christian any more than putting a radish in a bowl makes it a salad. You need to ask the hard questions before you decide to pursue her."

"Says the guy who started out all wrong with Sadie."

"Which gives me the right to caution you, man. I was on such uneven footing because I didn't ask God for guidance and then listen to Him. Pretty sure our road would have been much different if I had."

"But it turned out. You guys worked through all the junk and are happily engaged. Or so it looks like." Not that the perfectionist in Alex condoned the rocky route Peter and Sadie's relationship had traveled, but he desperately needed to deflect Peter.

"We are. And the next four months are going to be torture, waiting, but I totally get why Sadie wanted a long engagement. We're using the time to get to know each other and set our foundation deeper in God's word. Which brings me back to Marley."

Drat. There for a few seconds, Alex had seen reason to hope they could talk about how amazing Sadie was. Peter could rhapsodize forever about his fiancée's many virtues.

"She's been in church the past couple of weeks. That's a good start. But make sure you're on the same page."

Alex traced the edge of the table with his finger. "We've talked about God."

Peter leaned back in his chair. "And?"

"She wanted to know what my God was like."

"*Your* God? That's... odd."

"It was, kind of." Alex met Peter's gaze. "I told her. She seemed to think that God was all about judgment."

"Wow. I wonder what her background is."

"I don't know, but you're right. I need to find out." Was that the kind of conversation to have in a place like Antonio's? Knowing Tony, he'd go out of his way to set a romantic scene at their reserved table. Alex's dad and uncles had bought and renovated the old building along the river. They'd created multiple semi-private dining nooks for two, both on the main floor and on the roof, smug as only Italian romantics could be about their design input. Alex knew for a fact that his parents booked one of those every time Dad's flight schedule put him home for a couple of days.

Peter studied him for a long moment then nodded. "Been by to see Wesley and Kass's baby?"

Change of subject. Excellent. Alex shook his head. "A girl, I heard."

"Yeah. Newborns are sure tiny."

"I noticed that with Lillian." Alex quirked his brows at

his cousin. "And Eden and Jacob found out they're having twins. Are you getting baby fever?"

Peter's cheeks reddened as he surged to his feet and paced to the counter, where he poured another coffee. "All in good time."

Alex chuckled. "Sadie's looking good. She's lost a lot of weight."

Peter glared at him. "You're not supposed to notice."

"It would be hard not to notice those curves emerging."

"I'm proud of her. There's no way I could cut sugar right out of my life. I mean, she's figured out ways to still have sweets that taste pretty good, but it's a huge deal to her."

"And here I thought you supported her in every way."

"One hundred percent." Peter patted his flat abs. "Thankfully, I seem to have a fast metabolism and can eat whatever I want. I took it for granted before Sadie, but I definitely don't throw it in her face."

"You've always been active since we were kids. Basketball all the time. Your job with Fish and Wildlife. Now with Bridgeview Backyards. Makes a difference."

Peter nodded. "You'd better watch out, dude. You with that office job."

"Which is why I go by the gym a few mornings a week. I don't want to pack on the pounds."

"Besides, women dig muscles."

"Do they?" Alex asked blandly. "How many have you asked? Enough for statistical significance?"

"Didn't need to poll." His cousin grinned. "Experience, and all that."

"We should let Evan know to get his nose out of his textbooks occasionally."

Peter snorted. "He ran circles around you on the court during Hoopfest. Around both of us."

"He did, at that." Alex remembered the day the Bulldogs had celebrated in the bistro. One of the many times he'd noticed Marley. "Any advice for my big date tomorrow?" He couldn't believe he was asking.

"Never kiss on the first date."

That's where Alex had gone wrong with Linnea. One of many, like making sure she *wanted* to be kissed. She had not.

"Kidding, sort of. I did it. But, honestly, then I kind of regretted it."

"Because of the whole weird thing where you started dating her because you wanted her house."

Peter winced. "Yeah, that. Just don't put a ton of pressure on either of you tomorrow night. I get that you're going all out with Antonio's, but relax. Get to know her. Don't let the atmosphere inform your actions."

"Big talk," Alex said lightly. But kissing Marley would be pretty sweet, at least if she kissed him back. He'd been around enough of that kind of kissing to notice how it took a guy's knees out. Experiencing it for himself with a girl who was into him? Would be amazing.

"Well, you asked. I'm impressed, dude. All this talk about achieving the corner office before dating, yet here you are, talking about a girl with stars in your eyes."

"Stars?" He quirked an eyebrow. "Not me."

"Uh. Yeah. Keep telling yourself that." Peter gulped his coffee. "Oh, one more thing. Flowers. Women love flowers."

Alex hadn't even thought of that. "I wonder what kind..."

"Daisies."

"How would you know?"

"Dude. Haven't you looked at her paintings?"

The chickens' eyes stole all his attention.

"Trust me. She paints daisies everywhere."

Huh. "You might be right."

"Always, man. Don't forget it."

◦◦◦

THIS WAS SO FAR beyond Marley's dreams she must have tumbled into a fairy tale.

Antonio's was exquisitely patterned after a Mediterranean villa with Romanesque columns and arches and marble floors. But, instead of guiding them to one of the private dining alcoves they passed, the maître d' led them up a grand staircase to a rooftop patio.

Marley managed not to gasp out loud. From the street below, Antonio's looked like a two-story building, but reality was so much better. A windowed false front offered street-side privacy, but a slight breeze drew her gaze to the view of the Spokane River. Across the rapids, the riverbank rose sharply upward with the development of Kendall Yards perched on the overlook. Few windows over there seemed to have a view of Antonio's, though.

The fragrance of sun-warmed lavender wafted from planters. Tall potted plants and arches and trellises divided the rooftop into intimate nooks, more casual than the main floor.

Whew, because Marley had been feeling severely underdressed in her lacy T-shirt and her prettiest flowing skirt. She'd been caught off kilter the instant Alex appeared at her doorstep wearing slacks, a button-down short-sleeved shirt, and a tie, extending a vibrant bouquet of gerbera daisies with a shy smile. When she'd caught a whiff of his cologne, she'd nearly swooned. She was lucky if she didn't smell like chickens and acrylic paints, even after a long bubble bath.

The maître d' gestured to a narrow white-swathed table right against the clear panels overlooking the river. Both chairs faced the view.

"Thank you," Alex said to the maître d' then pulled one of the chairs for Marley.

The man bowed slightly. "Your waiter will be with you shortly."

"Thanks," whispered Marley, slipping onto the seat. As Alex settled beside her, she turned to peek at him. "This is... amazing."

The skin around his eyes crinkled when he smiled. "It turned out really well, didn't it? My dad and his brothers invested both cash and time into the renovation." A shadow crossed his face. "I only wish my uncle Al had lived to be part of it."

"Uncle Al? Who is he?"

"You've met Gabriella, right? Her dad. His truck was T-boned by a drunk driver a couple of years ago. He never regained consciousness."

"Oh, that's terrible!"

"Aunt Winnie has been a rock through it all, but it must be so hard. She just holds onto her faith that God knows what He's doing." Alex stared out across the river. "Gabby's the middle of five kids. It's been especially hard on the youngest two — Michael saw the accident happen just a block from the elementary school at the close of classes. He was eleven at the time."

Marley's heart went out to the boy. "I can't imagine."

She had her own horror stories, but she hadn't watched her father die. No, he'd managed that all on his own, in private.

The waiter arrived with embossed menus. "What may I get you to drink?"

Alex turned to her. "Would you like a glass of wine?"

She shook her head quickly. Alcohol was a bad idea if she wanted to keep her head. And she did. "Ice water, please."

"Same for me," he told the waiter, who nodded and backed away.

"You don't have to—"

"My family was big on a glass of wine with dinner, but that changed a couple of years ago."

"Because of your uncle?"

"Before that." He took a deep breath and turned to look at her again. "My brother Basil began drinking too much, and no one really caught the signs. He ran a police road-block one night and got slapped with a DUI and a month in jail."

Marley clapped her hand over her mouth. "Was anyone hurt?"

"No, thankfully. But Basil left Spokane after that and rarely returns for a visit. He moved to Seattle."

"Were you close?" She should have kept that in the present tense.

"Not as close as I am with Evan and Jasmine. Basil has always been a bit arrogant, ever since we were kids. I'm five years younger. Too big a gap for him to have noticed me as more than an annoyance."

"I can't imagine anyone looking down on you."

He quirked a grin at her. "Thanks. I guess I have my own brand of... I'd prefer to call it self-confidence. Anyway, we clash, so we don't hang out." He studied her for a few seconds. "You once told me you had a brother. Older or younger?"

Marley took a deep breath. The questions had to come eventually, but now? She opened her menu. "Older. We're not close, either." Now, that was an understatement. "We should choose our dinner before the waiter returns."

"You're right." Alex opened his as well. "You may notice that Tony offers a lot of low-carb choices. He's big on stuff like zucchini noodles as an option instead of pasta. He even has a couple of sugar-free desserts on the menu."

"The ketogenic diet is big right now. I guess that's why?"

"Probably. I know he's gotten some ideas from Sadie. She's not doing keto, exactly, but those options work for her diet."

"Ava's mom made a sugar-free dessert last Sunday. It tasted better than I expected."

Alex grinned. "Yeah, they're a little different, but not bad at all. Aunt Betta likes to support Sadie, which is great. And I'm sure you've heard Astrid's rants about sugar and junk food."

"She's something else. But she's been really helpful training me. I just had to get over her..."

"Opinions? Biases?"

"That works." Marley laughed. "So what do you recommend here?"

"Everything. My cousin is an amazing chef. I haven't tasted one dish Tony's created that I didn't want to have every single day afterward."

"High praise." Marley slid her finger down the menu. "Maybe the classic Fettucine Florentine."

"Mmm. You can't go wrong with that. I think I'll do the

Pasta Primavera. Would you like an appetizer? The Clams Oreganata are terrific."

"Oreg — what?"

"Clams baked in buttered bread crumbs seasoned with oregano and parsley."

Her mouth watered at the thought. "Sounds good."

Alex gave their order to the waiter and turned back to Marley. "Tell me about your brother."

Did she have to? "My stepbrother, really. He's a few years older, and he's a jerk." Marley stared down at the rapids, churning just like her gut. How perfect that she sat next to Alex, so she could avoid eye contact.

"Did you live with your mom or your dad?"

"Back and forth. Mostly my mom when I was little, but then—" She hesitated. "And then my dad when I was a teen. They were never married, so I never had a family like yours."

He pressed his shoulder against hers, lightly. "While having a large, close family has its problems, I am thankful for them. You must have felt so alone."

She nodded, tears prickling her eyes.

"When did you hear about Jesus?"

From family to religion in one heartbeat. Would politics be next? "My mom sent me to Sunday school with a neighbor. She sometimes went, too."

"What was *your* God like?"

Marley recognized her question turned back to her. She bit her lip. God had seemed just like Reverend Smith. "Always watching, waiting for me to mess up." Possibly looking for opportunities to trip her so she'd fall flat on her face. Then He'd point fingers at her.

"Is that what you still believe?" His voice was so, so quiet.

She shook her head slightly. "I don't know what to think. The God Pastor Tomas talks about is quite different. It... it expands my heart to think of a God who loves me. Who wants good things for me. Who forgives me and welcomes me into His family."

"He's a good, good Father," murmured Alex.

Marley turned to face him. "There was a song about that last Sunday."

"One of my favorites. It's like a foundational truth being reinforced. God is a good Father. It's who He is, and we're loved by Him."

"I'm finding that, but it's hard to get the old picture out of my mind."

"Ask Him to show you." Alex's gaze caught on hers.

"I have."

"Then He will."

If only she had that simple belief... but it was coming. Peace soaked into her. Everything had changed with Gram Renton's legacy. She had her own home, her own chickens for company, great neighbors — on one side, anyway — a job, a validated artistic outlet, and maybe a boyfriend. The evening sun warmed the water and riverbank and trees. Classical music drifted from unseen speakers.

Life was good and full of promise.

13

*A*lex opened the gate to Marley's backyard, still basking in the glow of a perfect dinner, a perfect evening, though the affogato for dessert may have been a mistake. His veins had pumped with adrenaline even before finishing up with sugar topped with espresso, but hey, he probably wouldn't have slept tonight, anyway.

Could this be love?

The last vestiges of a magnificent sunset hung in the dusky sky. The fragrance of flowers from a wooden planter beside the bottom step nudged at his senses. Not lavender like at Antonio's, but evening-scented stocks. Clucking hens surrounded their feet, and Marley crouched to scratch heads and croon baby-talk at them.

That was cool, so long as she didn't expect him to participate. He'd enjoyed watching them from his kitchen window at times and could see how she found them to be pleasant companions. And inspiration for her art.

He waited for her to rise then took both her hands in his. "Thanks for a great evening, Marley."

Kiss? Or not?

Her face was in shadow, her long curls cascading down her shoulders. She looked amazing. Fresh like petals after dew.

"Thanks for inviting me. I enjoyed it."

He took a deep breath. Why did guys have to do all the work figuring stuff like this out? "I hope we can do it again soon."

"I'd like that." She peeked at him from below long lashes.

See? Right here, it was different than with Linnea. Linnea had withdrawn during their date and never asked for more. And then he'd kissed her anyway, and when she hadn't responded, he'd pushed it. As though that would make a magical difference. It had not.

Marley sucked in her lower lip and looked down. She was waiting for him to decide.

Kiss? Or not?

Alex slipped his arms around her waist and tugged her closer. A hen squawked and scrambled out of the way.

Marley let out a little giggle.

He closed his eyes and savored the feel of her pressed against him as he lightly stroked her back.

She trembled at his touch and tilted her head to look at him.

Yes. Kiss.

Alex leaned down, his eyes never leaving hers. He'd give her a second or two to duck away if she wanted. Instead, her lips parted slightly as she met his gaze. He touched his mouth to hers and tasted a delicious surge of electricity.

A muffled snort came from the shadows.

Alex jerked upright as he scanned the area. If that was

Evan or one of the Santoro cousins, he'd kill him and string him up by the toenails.

Feet stomped across a wooden deck. A door slammed.

Marley let out a nervous laugh. "Kenji."

Of course the old guy had nothing better to do than spy on his pretty young neighbor. "Does he watch you a lot?" Because that was all kinds of unsettling.

"Some. But my beans are growing and soon he won't be able to see in my yard."

Alex chuckled. "Clever. But if he bothers you, tell me. I'll talk to him." Would he ever.

"Thanks, but I'm sure it's nothing." Marley looked up at him.

Wow, the mood had definitely been broken, but maybe it was for the best. Alex pressed his lips to Marley's forehead then let his hands catch hers again as he took a half step back. "If you're certain."

She nodded.

"Can I walk you to church tomorrow? And will you come to my parents' house for dinner?"

"I'd like that, only... will your grandmother be there?"

"Not sure. It depends on if she finds out you're coming or not." Alex bobbed his eyebrows then winked. "Eventually, she'll stop checking you out."

"She's fine. She just asks some strange questions."

"Nonna means well. She loves her grandkids and wants the best for all of us." He hesitated. "She wants to know if you're it."

Marley opened her mouth, closed it, and looked away.

What had he said? Oh, man. Sounded like he meant he was head over heels in love and needed to convince Nonna. That wasn't true. He'd only known Marley a few weeks.

This had been an amazing first date, but it was only that. They had a long way to go before he could start thinking about forever.

But, for the first time, forever had a face. And she was beautiful.

⌒ℓᴄ

MARLEY LISTENED to Alex drive his car into the carport next door. Heard the door shut, his footfalls on the back steps, the door to his house door open and close. Then she sagged to her knees on the too-long grass before toppling over onto her back. She lay, arms stretched wide, and stared up at the night sky as hens nestled next to her.

With the steep embankment behind her house to block city lights and both neighbors with outside lights off, the stars above were visible.

Why hadn't Alex kissed her again, properly, after Kenji had stomped inside? That little brush had been nowhere near enough.

It was amazing how different the quick sweep of his lips had been than any other kiss she'd ever received. It was the first time she hadn't been repulsed. Maybe she wasn't broken. She'd actually wanted more.

What was different about Alex? He was a gentleman, but more than that. It wasn't just his large, close family. It had to be his faith. God only knew she hadn't been exposed to kind men who followed Him before this neighborhood.

What had Alex said? *Ask Him.* He'd said it with the quiet assurance that God would answer her questions.

"God?" she whispered. "Alex told me You're good, that

You love me and died for me. That You're not just out to get me like Reverend Smith said."

What was the song they'd sung last week that Alex had mentioned? *Good, Good Father.* Marley pulled her phone out of her purse, tapped in a search, and played the video through. Then again. The reassuring words trickled into her thirsty soul. After three times, she set her phone to play other songs by the same artist.

Reverend Smith had to be wrong. He had to be blind to whom God really was... or else using his position to purposefully mislead and control others. That sounded more likely. Because wasn't it obvious in the night sky that God was loving and good? Wasn't it obvious in creation? Or how about in the death of Jesus? Why would Jesus give His life for other people if not from deep, deep love?

Memories of her earliest visits to Sunday school surfaced. They'd sang *Jesus Loves Me* and learned about Jesus blessing the children. She'd learned how the Christmas story led to the Easter story, and that both were about love.

Reverend Smith had come along later. Now, the final chains of his message of condemnation shattered from around Marley's heart. A judgmental God would not make such a huge, sacrificial overture. But a God of love? He offered a way for messed-up people to come to Him. She only needed to embrace it as she had as a small child.

"Thank You." Marley looked up into the quiet night. Was that a shooting star or a wink from God?

She'd take it as a wink.

⌒⌣

NOTHING DECLARED a new relationship in Bridgeview

more clearly than sitting together in church. Marley might not recognize the announcement, but Alex knew what was going on around him.

The grins and winks and nudges did not go unnoticed, but that didn't keep him from smiling at anyone and everyone. He couldn't have pinched back his happiness if he tried.

Nonna had studied the two of them in the church foyer before the service began. Alex had carefully kept his distance from Marley for a few seconds, making sure Nonna could see both his hands. Not that he cared what his grandmother thought, but if he could head her off at the pass before she decided to join them for Sunday lunch, he'd do it, for Marley's sake. Even without Nonna, he fully admitted his branch of the family was large, noisy, and intimidating.

Now Hailey North squeezed in at the end of the pew, and everyone scooted a little tighter to make room. Alex didn't mind having Marley pressed against him one bit.

Logan spoke into his microphone at the piano, inviting everyone to stand and sing *Good, Good Father*.

Alex grinned at Marley, and she smiled back before turning to read the words on the screen. Was it his imagination, or did he hear her sing out on the chorus?

Pastor Tomas soon announced this week's topic in the series of God's attributes. "God is good. He is infinitely kind and full of good thoughts toward His creation. Let me read today's text from The Voice. 'Taste of His goodness; see how wonderful the Eternal truly is. Anyone who puts trust in Him will be blessed and comforted.' That's from Psalm 34:8."

He looked out at the congregation. "Let those words seep into your heart. Trusting the Lord opens you up to receive His blessings. Even a little taste brings positive benefits, like stepping from the shadows into the light. Let's talk about goodness. Specifically, God's goodness."

Alex settled into his seat. This couldn't have come at a better time after the previous evening's conversation. He hadn't brought up the subject this morning as they'd walked the few blocks to church, but he'd sure been tempted. It was hard simply leaving the topic alone for the Holy Spirit to work with. He could pray now, though, as he had last night.

He kept a surreptitious eye on Marley. She sat with rapt attention, lips slightly parted as she drank in the sermon. By the end of the service, Alex felt sure his prayers were being answered. He was also certain he wanted to kiss her for real. Those pink lips drew him every time.

Later.

As the service closed, Evan socked him in the shoulder from the pew behind. When Alex turned, Evan's eyebrows shot into his dark hair as he flicked his gaze between Alex and Marley.

Alex grinned and nodded.

Evan rolled his eyes. By some miracle, he kept his mouth shut.

Ava and Marley carried on a whispered conversation, ending with his cousin flashing him a grin. Peter already knew. He must have told Sadie, since the two of them were singularly uncurious. Jasmine, however, edged against the tide from the back of the sanctuary, where she and Nathan had sat with the baby, her gaze fixed on Alex. But someone intercepted her to coo at Lillian.

Alex leaned closer to Marley. "Let's go."

She flashed him a smile. "Okay." She followed him out

the end of the pew away from his sister then he guided her to the back.

But exiting via the center aisle meant there was no getting away from Pastor Tomas.

Or from Nonna, who came bearing down like a freight train in a tunnel. Jasmine should take some lessons. Nonna's gaze swung between him and Marley a couple of times before she opened her mouth to speak.

Just then, Aunt Genevera caught Nonna's arm. "Mamma? Would you like me to give you a ride up to the house?"

"I was thinking of Raimondo—"

"Oh, no. Tieri will be so disappointed. She wanted to see you last week and show you her new costume for dance, but you didn't come."

Go, Aunt Gen.

"Well, in that case..." Nonna gave Alex one more look and turned away.

Aunt Genevera winked at Alex before catching her grandson, little Luca, into one arm. Taking Nonna's elbow with her other hand, she strolled away.

Marley let out a breath. "Close call."

Alex chuckled. "Yep. I owe my aunt one. Mom must have briefed her. But we aren't home free yet." He poked his chin toward the queue forming to talk to Pastor Tomas.

She nodded, as though she understood the requirement of shaking the pastor's hand before leaving. She really hadn't told him much about her former church. Just enough that he knew it wasn't a place he'd want to call his spiritual home.

Alex placed his hand on her lower back to guide her into the queue. Why couldn't he keep it there? Right. Gossip.

Everyone's minds would jump to conclusions that might be correct... albeit too early.

"Thank you." Marley gripped the pastor's hand. "I really appreciated your sermon this morning. It confirmed things I was thinking about just last night. How good God has been to me, even when I didn't always see His hand. I needed to hear what you had to say this morning."

Alex turned her way. She hadn't said anything about this to him. Not yet, anyway.

"God knows what we need to hear long before we do, so I'm glad to help." Pastor Tomas smiled at her then Alex. "Good to see you both here today."

There was a slight emphasis on the word *both*. Alex shook the man's hand with a smile. "Good to be here. I was reminded this week to be grateful for you and for Bridgeview Bible. Thank you for rooting us in God's word."

"It's my calling and my honor. It's Marley, right? Have you met my wife?" Pastor Tomas pulled his diminutive wife closer from where she chatted with someone else. "Marley, this is Juanita. You'd be welcome to stop by the church office sometime and talk to either of us if you have questions."

"Thank you. I'll keep that in mind."

"It's a pleasure to meet you, and I'll echo Tomas's invitation." Juanita grasped Marley's hand in both of hers. "I've popped into the bistro a couple of times in the past few weeks and seen you there, but didn't have a chance to introduce myself. And those chicken paintings are yours, right? You have a great talent."

"Thank you."

"It's good to see you around Bridgeview. It looks like you're settling in well?"

Marley's cheeks pinked.

Alex's hand found its way to the small of her back yet again. "We've been holding you up long enough, and we're expected at my parents' for dinner."

Pastor Tomas's eyes twinkled. "I wouldn't want to keep you from that. Maybe sometime you'll join us for Sunday lunch, instead."

Alex murmured something noncommittal and steered Marley away. It would get easier, right?

---

14

*A*lex held the gate open for her and swept his hand around. "Our community garden."

Marley stepped into a refreshing oasis and turned to him. "I had no idea this was here. I've walked within half a block dozens of times, but I guess this street isn't on my way anywhere."

He grinned at her and leaned closer. "I should remind you that's Nonna's house next door, but I'm pretty sure she's still at Uncle Franco and Aunt Gen's. Nonna donated this space to the community three years ago, and Linnea and Logan turned it into what you see."

What she saw was two rows of raised garden beds, bursting with a variety of plants, stepping up the shallow slope. The lot's edges overflowed with lush herbs and flowers alive with fluttering butterflies. A pebble fountain anchored a near corner, while a gazebo sat just beyond it. "This is amazing."

"It is pretty cool. I wish I could tell you I had something to do with it, but I didn't. Since so much of Bridgeview is on a steep, north-facing slope, this space allows a lot of residents to have a vegetable garden they couldn't otherwise have."

"Mine isn't doing so well." For one thing, Zephyr had staked the area out for dust baths. "You're right about the natural light and the rocky soil." Why hadn't she known about this garden before making her attempt? But it had probably been booked up months earlier.

"That's why Bridgeview Backyards does nearly everything in raised beds like the ones here." Alex grimaced. "Also, my yard has no trees to interfere with the sunshine we do get, and no one has to rake leaves."

Marley took a deep breath. "I like my bushes and trees. I should probably plant a hedge on Kenji's side. What grows quickly?"

"I'm not the expert, but I'm sure Jasmine could tell you. The pole beans are genius, though."

"If they all germinated and grew. Right now, it's only obvious I'm trying to get privacy with the wire mesh, but the beans are unlikely to fill it in. Unless they branch out a lot?"

He shook his head. "I know enough to tell you pole beans grow in a single vine."

Drat. She should have done more homework. "Well, I tried. Next year, I'll have something else in place. Something better."

Alex turned to her and tucked a long curl behind one ear.

Her cheek tingled from his touch, and she met his gaze. Was he finally going to finish what he'd started last night before Kenji interrupted? But Alex just searched her face.

He seemed like a take-charge kind of guy, so why wasn't he doing more than stare?

Marley cupped his face in both hands and felt him stiffen. Okay, she'd been wrong. Wrong about everything. But before she could mumble an apology and pull back, his hands rested on her waist.

"Marley," he whispered.

"Alex?" Breathless, she fingered the short curls at the nape of his neck as her gaze drifted from his blue eyes to his pink lips. If he didn't...

He did.

Alex's fingers caught in the long curls behind her neck. With one searching look, he bent closer, his lips skimming hers.

She tried to catch them, but he feathered kisses across her cheeks, her nose, her forehead, her eyelids. Heat flared across her face with every gossamer touch and surged through her body until her knees weakened. Marley cupped her hands on the back of his head and tried to still his teasing mouth with her own.

There.

That was better. The reality surpassed the fantasies that had tantalized her all night long. He smelled of the cologne she'd begun to associate with him. Tasted of the honey-laced struffoli they'd had for dessert at his parents' house earlier. Sight and sound were gone, unheeded. Unneeded.

Only touch and taste remained. What a sensation they brought. She could lose herself here, where Alex's hands caressed her back, where his body pressed against hers, where his lips captivated hers.

Too soon, he pulled back, resting his forehead against

hers. "Marley, you take my breath away." His voice was soft, yet rough. Full of emotion, full of wonder.

Her eyes drifted open, and she clutched him closer. "More," she whispered.

Alex chuckled softly. "Maybe better not." He kissed her lightly.

She held back a groan, but he was doubtless right.

Someone coughed.

Marley stiffened. Not again. Was it Marietta? She didn't even want to look, but if it were Alex's nonna, there'd doubtless be words.

"Hiya, Hailey," said Alex easily.

Oh, no. Marley's other boss. Hailey ruled the kitchen at Bridgeview Bakery and Bistro. In Kass's absence, Shay and Ava ran the floor, so Marley didn't have a lot to do with Hailey, but still.

She took a deep breath and turned, thankful that Alex's arms didn't drop away. "Hi, there."

"How about that? Alex and Marley. Quick moving, guys." Hailey shook her head, a lopsided smirk on her face. "And, Alex, I thought you were waiting to get involved with anyone until you had that corner office in the bag? Did I miss a chance to congratulate you?"

Alex chuckled, but it sounded forced. Marley peeked a glance at the tight lines around his eyes. Uh oh. "Not yet."

Wait. A corner office? They hadn't talked much about his job, but how had Marley not clued in that he was so corporate minded? But, yeah. He went to work every day in slacks, a button-down shirt, and a tie. Carrying a briefcase.

He was a responsible man with a career in accounting. Had to be a good thing, right? So unlike her. She'd barely squeaked through high school — especially math — and had ricocheted from one dead-end job to the next ever since, struggling to find her place in life.

"Well, sorry for interrupting. I was looking for a place to kick back for a while, but I'll go down to the river instead." Hailey rocked back on her heels.

"It's fine. We were just leaving." Alex's fingers threaded through Marley's, and he guided her toward the gate.

Marley glanced back to find her boss still watching them. "See you Tuesday!" she called.

Hailey nodded, an inscrutable expression on her face.

When they were half a block away, Marley turned to Alex. "What's her problem?"

Alex shook his head. "Jealousy? But not because of me," he added hastily. "Because she's tried to snag nearly every unattached man in Bridgeview at one time or another. I don't know why she's so desperate."

"Did you ever ask her out?"

"No way. She's a couple of years older than me and *so* not my type. But pretty much all her friends are married now, and Kass just had a baby, so I guess she's feeling it even more these days."

Marley got it. Sometimes it felt like everyone else's life was on track and hers... was not. But with her own home and selling two paintings — and now, with Alex's interest — maybe she was finally on her way. That and feeling the presence of God for really the first time in her life. "Sounds like you haven't dated much?" She swung Alex's hand as they headed down the sidewalk.

"Not much." He shot her a sideways glance. "Hailey's right that I've been pretty focused on my career. I've got goals and a five-year plan."

She'd have pulled her hand away if he'd let her.

He quirked a grin at her. "Sometimes plans need adjusting. I'm sure yours changed when you got the news about Gram Renton's place."

"I didn't really have any before that," Marley admitted. "Survival."

"Oh?"

That was an era best forgotten. "But now I'm hoping to sell more paintings. Wesley came by the bistro the other day and said he'd be willing to coach me on the business side of art." Because numbers were *so* not her thing.

"I could do that."

Marley raised her eyebrows at him.

"I'm an accountant. I can set up your books if that would help."

"Right. I think there's other things he meant. Like working with galleries."

"Is being an artist what you aspire to?"

She tried to read something into his bland question, but couldn't quite put a finger on it. "Art makes me happy, especially the new direction with the chickens. It's hard to explain, but I get in this zone and everything else falls away. I'd be late for work every single day if I didn't set five alarms."

His eyebrows shot up. "Seriously?"

"Yeah?" Why was that weird? "Haven't you ever gotten so wrapped up doing something else you showed up late to work?"

"But it's my job. My responsibility."

"A job you chose, sounds like. Working at the bistro isn't like that for me. It's great because I can be around people and make them happy and get paid for it. But the art and the chickens and the garden are where it's at."

"If you ever need a hand weeding out that yard, let me know."

"Those are herbs and flowers. The chickens love them." Marley looked up at him, eyebrows raised. "*I* love them." Although there were definitely a few plants she hadn't catalogued yet.

Alex's mouth — the one that had sent her into rapture moments ago — shifted slightly. "It is very... vibrant."

When he didn't say more, she pressed on. "I don't want a sterile yard like yours, Alex. I mean, I get that you and Peter are running a business with it, and that's cool. But that's not for me. I need something more inspirational. Eclectic."

He stared ahead as they navigated up the sidewalk between the community center and the basketball court. "You're right. My career is everything to me. I mean, not more than God, but more than just about everything else. I worked two jobs and lived with my parents to save up money for a down payment on my place."

"That's..." What word was she looking for? It was intense. Focused. She settled for "admirable."

"Admirable?" His eyebrows spiked as he looked at her.

"Well, yes. You obviously know what you want and then go get it. That's commendable." Did he want her? Did she want to be wanted by a man with that kind of fixation?

On the one hand, it definitely offered security like she'd never known in all her twenty-four years. On the other, it sounded maybe just a teensy bit dull. His kisses were far from boring, but they couldn't kiss all the time. Too bad.

"Such a rousing sentiment," he said with a teasing lilt.

Whew. She'd wondered for a minute if she'd been too unappreciative. But really, she didn't know enough about her own freedom to evaluate if Alex's penchant for order worked for her or not.

Should she be dating a man if she didn't know? But that was what dating was for, right? To get to know each other. To find out if they were compatible.

Alex swung their hands between them then, with a grin, bumped her shoulder.

She focused on the feel of his fingers twined with hers, his warm palm against hers. How could a simple touch offer security? So they had some differences. No two people were alike, and wouldn't it be boring if they were?

"I was thinking of something more casual for our next date. That is, if you'd like to go out again."

He had to ask? Marley squeezed his fingers. "I'd love to. What do you have in mind?"

His grip tightened, too. "Depends. Do you enjoy bike riding? You could borrow Jasmine's if you don't have one. There are a lot of good bike trails around here. Or, we could visit Manito Park. They have some formal gardens and other more casual areas. Or, there's—"

"Manito Park sounds lovely."

"Okay, great. Is Saturday good again?"

So far away? But a week would go quickly. "Sure. I get off at five."

Alex shot her a grin. "I'll pack a picnic and pick you up from the bistro?"

"It sounds fun." And now she was going to lie awake tonight wondering what a guy like him would bring for a picnic.

And how she got to be so lucky.

15

*S*orry, I can't work late tonight. I have a date." He had plans most nights these days.

Mr. Sanderson's eyebrows rose as he drilled Alex's eyes. "Not optional, Santoro. We can't afford to lose this client, and he's under a time crunch for these reports. We're all here until probably ten o'clock."

Alex hadn't signed up for this. Not since he and Marley had been spending so much time together the past couple of weeks. He opened his mouth to stand his ground, but his boss had already pivoted away. "Every night this week, Santoro. You, too, Jovanic, Bristol. Any plans you had are canceled effective immediately."

Alex exchanged a look with his coworkers as their boss exited the lunch room.

"You heard the man. Break's over." Nelson Bristol gulped the last of his coffee as he surged to his feet.

"He can't really do this, can he?" Alex turned to Clint.

The other man shook his head as he rinsed his mug. "I think he can. Have you forgotten this isn't the first time?"

"Well, true, but still. It seems to be happening more often." Maybe he just hadn't noticed because he hadn't had plans until recently. Devoted company man and all that.

"Sandy's going to kill me," muttered Clint. "Her sister invited us over tonight, and Sandy made me promise not to miss it. She's going to think I'm faking to avoid her family."

"Then go home." Alex was debating the wisdom of doing the same. Marley would say she understood, but would she really? She still seemed fragile, their relationship new. Telling her he had to work overtime would only 'prove' he'd rather be at work than with her.

Far from true, but her insecurities ran deep.

"Dude. If I say no to the extra work, I'm kissing this job goodbye. We'll lose our house and car, and Sandy won't be any happier with *that* scenario. I'm picking my battles." Clint strode out.

Alex needed this job, too. His first task was to keep Mr. Sanderson happy so he'd remember that lure he'd cast back when Alex was a newbie with the firm. *Work hard, Santoro, and when my VP retires in a few years, you should be ready to replace him. We could use a young guy with a lot of energy in that position.*

That corner office had a great view of downtown Spokane and the river, but what was a view when he could explore the real thing with Marley? He could give that energy to Mr. Sanderson, or he could use it to live life.

"You still in here, Santoro? I need those files on my desk before you leave. They'll determine where we take the search from here."

"Why take on such a rush job when we don't have the manpower?" Alex held his breath. He'd never challenged his boss before.

Sanderson's eyes drilled Alex. "I thought you were hungry, Santoro. Eager to prove your worth."

"I am." Or, he had been.

"Do you have any idea how many resumes hit my inbox every single day? Trust me. I won't have any trouble replacing you if needed." His eyebrows rose. "Any questions?"

"I understand, sir. I'll get right back to the report."

"I thought you'd see it my way."

Alex brushed past and headed toward his cubicle. The whole semi-open area was silent but for the clicking of computer keys and the occasional squeak of a desk chair.

Was this really what his life had become? Just keeping Mr. Sanderson happy, no matter what it took? It had all seemed reasonable for the first couple of years. With the overtime hours came overtime pay, and that had helped fund the down payment on his house. Then it had enabled him to invest in Bridgeview Backyards.

This job kept him from worry about the future. Sure, God had promised to supply all his needs, and He'd done that with this job. It was up to Alex to keep it.

On to running that next report, then. When Mr. Sanderson wasn't watching him quite so closely, he'd text Marley and let her know they were off for tonight. She'd understand. Right?

❧

MARLEY SAT on her back steps in the gathering darkness with Chloe and Gloria on her lap and the other three crouched nearby. Sometime before winter, she'd need a shelter for them, but there was lots of time to think of that.

She should save up a bit from every paycheck. Then it wouldn't feel like such a hit when the need arose.

Alex still wasn't home, unless she'd somehow missed him. Wouldn't he see her outside and come say goodnight? Unless his text had been meant to put her off. She could see an accountant working overtime in tax season, but what could possibly be so important in summer? Was he tired of hanging out with her and just didn't know how to tell her?

That didn't sound like Alex.

They'd spent a lot of time together in the past few weeks. Saturday night dates. Sunday dinners with his family. More recently, evening walks down along the river.

No, he wouldn't offer a flimsy excuse not to see her. He was honest. Direct.

Marley shifted on the wooden step. Gloria fluttered her wings and grumbled before settling back down. She smoothed Chloe's feathers, and the hen leaned into her touch.

This was why Marley should have stuck with her chickens. They had no expectations beyond a few snuggles, cool water, and some fruit and veggies. In response, they gleefully provided her with eggs. A simple relationship.

Alex was not simple.

Most things worth having weren't. They needed maintenance. Trust. Give and take. In all her twenty-four years, she'd seen few relationships that stood the test of time. None, really, before moving to Bridgeview. Now she'd been introduced to people like Alex's parents, who'd been together for over thirty years, at her best guess, looking at the ages of Alex's siblings. Ava's parents, too.

It was almost enough to give a girl hope until she remembered where she'd come from. Mom and her drinking problem. Dad's drugs. Brandon... no. Not going there.

She was free of them all. Gram Renton had unlocked Marley's chains. Or God had. Either way, she wasn't going back. She'd had a glimpse of a new future. A new, stronger, Marley inhabited it, no longer a victim at anyone's whim.

Not Alex's, either. She wouldn't depend on him. She couldn't. His text tonight was only a small letdown, but still a great reminder she was getting in over her head. Too many of her thoughts revolved around him, definitely encouraged by Ava and Gabby at work, who seemed thrilled to have a front-row seat to Marley's romance with their cousin.

She nudged Chloe and Gloria off her lap and rose.

No more waiting for Alex. Not tonight. Not ever. This girl was going to stand on her own two feet. Hanging out with her chickens and painting them. Working at the bistro to get her people fix and buy some extras. Maybe church. Maybe not. That last sermon had been on the holiness of God and seemed to come a little close to Reverend Smith's proclamations.

Maybe she should talk to Juanita or Pastor Tomas about that.

∽

"COME PLAY BASKETBALL WITH US." Oren tugged at Marley's hand.

"Sounds fun." Marley put her other arm around Arie's shoulder and followed the boys out of Alex's parents' house.

Alex stood there, staring after them, hands spread. "What just happened?"

"Guess you're too old for her, after all." Jasmine smirked, handing Lillian off to Nathan.

"No, seriously." His forehead furrowed as he narrowed his eyes. He'd barely seen Marley what with all the overtime last week... and there was more of that to come. He thought she'd be as glad to spend time with him today as he was to be with her. And in a month of joining his family for Sunday dinner, she'd never agreed to shoot hoops with his nephews.

"You could get out there and join them." Nathan lifted the baby to his shoulder and patted her back as Jasmine disappeared into the kitchen.

"I could..." Alex dragged the word out. "But doesn't this seem odd to you?"

"How's that? She sees you all the time, right? So she's trying to fit into the family. Seems positive to me."

"You don't understand."

Lillian burped, and Nathan expertly wiped her mouth before repositioning her. "Okay. So try me."

"I've worked a lot of overtime this week. Had to cancel plans with Marley twice."

"Ouch."

The thumping of the basketball on the driveway came faintly through the door. A few seconds later, Oren whooped. Nice someone was having fun.

"Yeah, my boss laid down the law. We've all been working fourteens."

Nathan's eyebrows shot up. "That's crazy."

"I know. One of our major clients is taking over another company and there seem to be some inconsistencies in their books. We've been going through everything with a fine-toothed comb to find the problem." Books. What a misnomer. They'd used the shoebox method, in this day and age of spreadsheets and QuickBooks. No excuse, really.

"Oh, man."

Sympathy. Just the way Alex liked it. "I want to keep Sanderson happy, but this is seriously interfering with my life. Must be nice to work for yourself and create your own schedule."

Nathan guffawed. "I can tell you haven't freelanced. In advertising, anyway, clients come and go. Keeping the right balance is a never-ending juggle. I have to work enough to meet the financial needs of my wife and daughter while *not* working so much I avoid their other needs. You're not the only one juggling challenges, man."

"I guess." Did he really think he was that unique? Sanderson had fed him the belief he was special enough to become a VP if he only stayed loyal and worked his butt off. Alex was beginning to think it had only been a well-set hook on a long fishing line.

"Don't like your hours? Don't like your boss? Quit. Find something else. A guy with your creds should have no trouble landing a better job."

"The thought has crossed my mind a couple of times lately."

Nathan jabbed Alex's arm. "At least you can get away from your boss. I share skin with mine." He laughed.

Alex rolled his eyes. "Funny. You could get an office job if you wanted."

"Probably. But even with all the hassle of entrepreneurship, I still prefer working for myself. You could do it, too. Hang out your shingle. Work from home."

"Tempting, but I don't think so."

Nathan studied him. "Because you need your boss to stroke your ego?"

Alex reared back. "Hey, what's that supposed to mean?" He didn't care about that. Did he? The view from the corner office flitted through his mind. Okay, so he did care.

"Just wondered. Then all I've got is to pray about it, but I'm sure you have been. God will give you a clear path if you're asking for it. Watching for it."

He hadn't been praying a lot. More like whining to himself about time lost with Marley... while applauding the extra padding for his bank account.

The door flew open, and Marley rushed in, clutching her phone, eyes wide.

"Are you okay?" She didn't look okay. He reached for her.

"I... Gram Renton passed away."

Alex gathered Marley close and smoothed her tangled hair. "I'm sorry." Not that she really knew the old woman. She'd only gone to visit once that Alex knew of, but Gram had been too far gone into dementia to know anyone.

Marley pushed at his arms for a little space. "There's no real funeral since she had no family, but the nursing home is having a memorial on Thursday morning. I want to go."

Alex nodded, not sure what to say.

"It's crazy." She blinked away a tear. "I didn't know her at all, but she turned my life around. I owe her everything."

Alex managed a chuckle. "You're confusing her with God."

"It sounds like that, doesn't it?" She dabbed moisture from her cheek and shook her head. "I don't know how to process this, but I need to attend. Say goodbye."

"I wish I could go with you, but I already know I can't

get time off work." Okay, he didn't really *want* to go to a stranger's memorial, but he hated to see Marley disheveled. In tears.

She looked up at him. "Can you try?"

"You don't understand. My boss has made it super clear that no one is getting any time off until this project is wrapped up."

"Maybe you'll be done by Thursday."

Alex rubbed Marley's arms. "I doubt it. I'm sorry."

"But—" She pursed her lips and turned away.

Helplessness rolled over him. He was a fixer, but he couldn't solve Sanderson's problem and he couldn't solve Marley's. What was the use of trying?

arley opened the door to the second bedroom then leaned against the doorframe, taking in the sight of dozens of boxes stacked precariously on old furniture and in the corners. Had Gram packed away her life by herself years ago, or had someone helped her more recently? That someone would want to know the old woman had passed on, most likely.

There was a lot of stuff in here, considering the house had been fully furnished with mismatched dishes still in the cupboards. Marley had so few of her own things, she'd gladly accepted the eclectic mix. A few pieces needed replacing sometime, like the lumpy, saggy sofa. Mostly, though, if it was good enough for an elderly woman, it was good enough for Marley.

Was this the room her dad had inhabited as a teen? How many kids had Gram fostered? Maybe there were clues in some of these boxes. She couldn't just haul them to the curb on trash day without knowing what she was tossing, could she?

No, her curiosity was too strong for that, especially after thinking of her dad. He'd rarely spoken of his years in foster care, and his adult life had followed a similar wandering pattern. Never quite belonging, never quite finding permanence.

Marley blinked stinging tears away. She wanted more than the sum of her experience. She'd found it in Jesus. "God? You are the *more* I was looking for."

She unhooked the flaps of the nearest cardboard box, and dust puffed into the air. Inside, a stack of papers appeared to be envelopes stuffed with receipts. Old bills. Nothing that could possibly have any worth. She set it aside and reached for the next box, this one full of embroidered tea towels and other linens yellowed with age.

Could they be salvaged? Made into anything useful? She smoothed the wrinkles enough to study the floral patterns labeled with the days of the week. Could they be turned into curtains for the kitchen, maybe? The yellow gingham ones hanging there now drooped lifelessly, but these would perk up the space. She'd need a sewing machine. For now, she'd wash them and see what they looked like without creases and wrinkles. Not that she had an iron.

Did Alex? Were his crisp clothes hand-pressed? She wouldn't put it past him.

Marley had just set the box in the corner of the kitchen to deal with later when she heard a knock at the door. Through the window, she spotted Jasmine with the baby in a carrier across her chest.

She pulled the door open. "Hi!"

"Hey! I wasn't sure if you were home or wanted company, but I was next door weeding and thought I'd stop in and see."

"Sure. Come on in. I was just going through old boxes in the spare room, but I'm glad to take a break. Would you like some iced tea?"

"Sounds good, but I don't want to interfere with your plans." Curiosity shone on Jasmine's face as she came in and closed the door behind herself. "What do you mean, old boxes?"

"I told you yesterday Gram Renton passed away. She'd left one of the bedrooms stuffed with old furniture and boxes. I've avoided that room since I moved in, but now that she's gone, it seems I should go through things and — I don't know — deal with it all."

"I'm sorry." Jasmine's brow furrowed in sympathy. "From what you've said, you didn't really know her. I'm not sure if that makes it easier or harder to go through her things."

"I'm not sure, either. It feels like an invasion of privacy, but it seems even worse to get rid of everything without looking." Marley poured tea into two mismatched glasses and set them on the small wooden table. She settled into the more rickety chair as Jasmine sat around the corner.

"Do you want a hand?" Jasmine took a sip of the tea. "I don't have anywhere else to be for a couple of hours. Maybe you have a place I could lay Lillian down. On your bed or somewhere?"

Marley stared at Alex's sister. "Really? You'd do that with me? For me?"

"Sure, why not? A big job like that is far more fun when shared with a friend." She grinned at Marley. "And I'd like us to be friends."

"I, um..."

Jasmine laughed. "It's cool you're dating my little brother, but you're also a new resident of Bridgeview and work for Kass and Hailey, who've been my friends forever. So you don't have to think of me as Alex's sister if that makes you uncomfortable."

A friend. Just... a friend. Ava said she wanted that, too, but she worked at a dance studio evenings after a full day at the bistro. She didn't have much extra time to hang out. Marley couldn't remember the last time she'd had real friends just for friendship's sake. "I'd like that."

"Cool. What have you found so far?"

"Oh!" Marley jumped up and grabbed the box. "Look at these. I wondered if I could make curtains for that window with them." She unfolded the Tuesday tea towel, gave it a flick, and held it out for Jasmine's inspection.

"Ooh. Love it." Jasmine glanced at the window then reached to finger the towel's corner. "It would totally work in this kitchen. One for every day of the week?"

Marley nodded.

"Sounds like a fun project. Do you sew?"

"Of course not. But I'll learn how."

Jasmine grinned. "I take all my sewing to Nonna. She helps me... when she doesn't take over, which is usually fine with me."

Big help. Marley sighed.

"I'm sure she'd give you a hand."

"Your grandmother terrifies me."

"Really? I know she's rather straightforward..."

"Is that what you call it? I feel like she's dissecting me with her eyes."

"I guess I can see that." Jasmine studied her. "She's a mama bear when it comes to her grandkids, wanting the best for each of us. She's a little protective." Her hand rubbed the curve of her small daughter's back in the carrier.

Marley draped the tea towel across the dusty box. Time to change the subject. "There are tons of boxes and a few pieces of furniture. It might all be garbage. So hard to know."

Jasmine took a long drink of the iced tea as she stood. "Show me where to lay Lillian and let's have a look."

An overture of friendship? Marley would take it with gratitude.

∂‑ℓ‑ℓ

ALEX HAD BEEN WATCHING for Marley to come out to her yard. At dusk, he'd given up, come to her door, and knocked.

She stood there with tendrils escaping her low ponytail, a smudge of dirt on her cheek, and an unraveled hem on her top.

"Uh... is this a bad time?" He shifted from foot to foot. Could she tell that her unkempt appearance caught him off guard? And yet it was past nine at night, and he hadn't texted ahead. He could be lucky she wasn't in pajamas. That she answered the door at all.

"No, it's fine. Come on in." She stepped back.

"Just for a minute." A few dirty dishes sat by the sink, boxes were stacked by the living room doorway, and a pile of unfolded linens covered the table. He'd obviously come at a bad time. A time when bohemian had given way to chaos. "I don't want to keep you from whatever you were doing." Probably cleaning, so she could sleep.

She smiled slightly. "Going through Gram's things in the spare room. Your sister gave me a hand for a while today. Yesterday, too."

Jasmine? She hadn't said anything, not that he'd seen her. He tried not to let his surprise show. "That's cool." He hoped.

She glanced at the clock, and her eyebrows arched. "I didn't realize how late it was getting. You just got home?"

"A bit ago." Why did this feel so awkward? "I just wanted to see how you're doing and tell you again I'm sorry about Thursday." Although going to a memorial for a woman he didn't know would have been weird, but he'd have done it for Marley. "Can you get the time off with Kass on maternity leave?"

She nodded. "Everyone is making it happen. Gabby is working straight through, and I'll pick up her closing shift. Astrid will stay longer, too." She blinked hard, shaking her head.

Tears? Maybe she had more grief over Gram Renton's death than she'd let on before.

"It's just... nowhere I've ever worked before would have done that. Figured out how to cover for each other, and do it with a smile on their faces. Like family."

She had low standards for family, but Alex already knew that. "That's what family and friends do." Jasmine getting to know Marley — which hat was she wearing?

"It's new to me." She dabbed at a tear and left a smear of dirt beneath her eye.

"Here." He wiped the smudge with his thumb.

She leaned into his touch, but Alex hesitated for a second before slipping his hands around her and drawing her close. Good thing he'd changed out of his office clothes in favor of shorts and a T-shirt. Laundry time was at a premium along with everything else.

He pressed a kiss to her forehead, tasting the dust and

sweat. He really shouldn't have come over without texting first, so she'd have had time to clean up if she wanted to. But that was the big question. It didn't seem like she cared about that so much.

"I should let you go." He slid his hands down her arms as he took a small step backward. "You probably have a few things to wrap up tonight. A shower and all that."

Marley studied him. Trying to figure him out, maybe?

Well, he was trying to figure *her* out, too. He hadn't been in her kitchen before, just on the doorstep when he picked her up. Surely, she usually kept it cleaner. The mess was only because of the big sorting job. He needed to give her the benefit of the doubt.

Alex gave her a soft, short kiss then let go of her hands. "Good night."

She wrapped her arms across her chest as though to warm herself, though the July evening was plenty warm. "Good night, Alex."

He let himself out of her house, aware of her gaze glued to his back. He stumbled over a hen on the back step, twisting his ankle before regaining his balance. Stupid chicken, wandering all over at night, where an owl could swoop in and grab her. Marley should know better. There wasn't even a coop. What was she going to do come winter?

Alex walked the long way around to his own backdoor just in time to catch sight of Peter mounting the steps on his return from Sadie's on the other side. Alex paused a moment to let his cousin enter the house. He didn't really feel like talking to anyone.

When he slowly climbed the steps, careful to tread quietly, he was startled to find Peter sitting on one of the two lawn chairs on the small back deck. "Hey. Didn't see you there."

There was just enough light glowing from the kitchen window to illuminate his cousin's grin. "Saw you coming up the drive. How are things?"

"Busy at work." But Peter already knew that.

"Right... how about with Marley?"

I don't want to talk about it. But if those words were spoken, they'd sound petulant. Childish. "Not sure."

"I get that."

"Is Sadie... tidy?"

His cousin laughed. "What kind of question is that?"

Alex settled onto the other chair. "Curiosity."

"So either Marley is a neat freak or a disaster. And if she were a neat freak, you wouldn't mention it, because you wouldn't even notice, since everything would be just how you like it."

"I asked about Sadie," Alex said through gritted teeth.

"Well, now that she's off junk food, she's better, since there aren't wrappers and pizza boxes everywhere. And she works long hours, so her place isn't always spotless. But she usually takes a couple of hours on Saturday to put things in order." Peter raised his eyebrows at Alex. "And now, back to Marley."

"I just popped by, and her place is a hot mess. More than simply a few things not put away."

"And this bothers you."

Alex sighed. "Yes. It does."

"Is it bad enough that it smells? Should city sanitation get involved?"

"Of course not. She's in the middle of clearing out the stuff Mrs. Renton left behind. Sorting it all."

"Sounds like a mess is reasonable at this stage?" There was a lilt of a question there.

"I guess. Maybe. But there's stacks of stuff everywhere. Wouldn't a reasonable person deal with them one at a time?"

Peter guffawed. "Apparently an Alex Santoro would, but I'm not sure he defines a *reasonable person*."

"Thanks."

"I'm only half kidding, cuz. You do know you're a bit OCD, right?"

"Because I like things in order?"

"Because you *demand* them in order. Alphabetical or numerical."

"So I'm hard to live with."

"Didn't say that. I like order myself. If I hated it so much, I wouldn't have lasted as your housemate for two years. Also, I won't be shocked to discover I take over a lot of the housekeeping duties when Sadie and I are married. It's possible I will care more than she does about the daily stuff."

Alex forced himself to settle his bristles. "There's piles of stuff everywhere at Marley's house. Unwashed dishes. She's covered with dust and dirt and sweat." And here was the stickler. "She didn't even seem to notice."

Peter's eyebrows shot up. "You show up at nine-thirty in the evening unannounced, and she should apologize to you that she's been working?"

"When you put it that way, it sounds terrible."

"Yeah. It does." He narrowed his gaze at Alex. "Listen, man. I'm no expert on relationships, but I do know a couple of things. One is that you can't expect the other person to change for you."

"But Sadie's lost a pile of weight."

"Dude. You know better. She didn't lose it *for me*. She started that journey independently of us dating. She wanted to be healthy *for herself.* Because *she* deserves it. Not because I do."

Alex closed his eyes. He knew that. So what was his problem? "Who does the changing, then?"

"Both, really. It's called growing up."

If he excused himself now, it would prove Peter's point. But, man, he sure wanted to. Alex swallowed hard. "I don't know if this is what's right for me. If Marley is the one, you know? We're so different. Is it worth it? Is *she* worth it?"

"I can't answer that, but I can sympathize. You remember what it was like for me last summer."

"Yeah. I remember."

"So here's the thing. You barely know Marley. Your first few dates are hardly in the rearview mirror, and now your schedule is crazy. So, relax. There's no rush. No need to make a snap decision tonight. Unless you *know* you're wrong. Otherwise, take it slow and ask the Lord to guide you both."

Alex shook his head. "I just don't like not knowing what's going on. This feeling of unsettledness."

"It's called anticipation." Peter chuckled. "Remember that rope swing out by the swimming hole when we were kids?"

"Yeah?"

"I loved that thing. The exhilaration of grabbing hold, leaping out, and letting go at just the right instant. Making the biggest splash I could."

Lazy childhood summer days replayed in Alex's memory. "I remember. I hated the queasy feeling in my gut of what might happen if I didn't nail it. If I let go too late and crashed back into the tree."

"But you never did. You jumped anyway."

Mostly because Basil had taunted him. At least his brother wasn't here now poking fingers at Marley. "So you think I should jump in with both feet."

"Not exactly. But get more than your little toe wet. See if Marley is the right woman or not. Messy isn't everything. Give her a chance."

17

*T*he week went by. Marley made her way via transit across the city for Gram Renton's memorial. The home's chaplain spoke briefly, and a few of the residents offered memories of her life. An elderly woman sat at a keyboard and led the group in singing *In the Garden*.

Gram would have liked those lyrics.

I come to the garden alone, while the dew is still on the roses...

Like Marley, Gram must have enjoyed the early morning in the wildflower-strewn yard. Maybe she'd communed with God the way the song said.

And he walks with me, and he talks with me, and he tells me I am his own, and the joy we share as we tarry there, none other has ever known.

Yes, there was intimacy in the garden at daybreak. Marley had taken to reading her Bible app on the back step with the hens clustered around her. She'd found a series of devotionals about God's love that quieted her doubts.

He speaks, and the sound of his voice is so sweet the birds hush their singing; and the melody that he gave to me within my heart is ringing.

She entered the bistro just past the busy lunch hour to see Kass behind the counter and Wesley, holding the baby, talking to her.

Oh, no. Marley hadn't meant for her boss to break her maternity leave for this event. "I'm so sorry..."

"Hi, Marley." Wesley turned with an easy grin. "Have you seen our princess lately?"

Marley peeked at the infant in the pink romper. "She's gotten so big!"

"A month old already," Kass said with an indulgent smile. "And don't worry about me. I just came in to help cover the lunch rush. I'm on my way home now that you're here."

"But Gabby..."

"She's here. It's fine, Marley. I had some office work to do, and just stayed a little longer to help out. Don't tell Wesley or Eleanor, but I kind of miss coming in."

Wesley chuckled like it was no big shock to him. "You should come by sometime soon, Marley, before Kass returns to work full time and I'm juggling Eleanor with my work schedule."

"I thought we were getting a part-time nanny." Kass eyed her husband.

He lowered his voice conspiratorially. "Only after Astrid gives up on the thought that she's the natural first choice."

Astrid was Wesley's ex's mom. Their relationship was likely smoother since the woman who connected them was dead, but still. Marley worked with Astrid every day. The woman was intense, to say the least. Marley could only imagine how Wesley and Kass wouldn't want her in charge of the baby. Never mind that Kass would need to replace her at the bistro.

"We'll find someone else and not even tell her until it's a done deal." Kass turned to Marley. "But he's right that you should come by and talk about business with him. I sold another of your paintings this morning."

Marley swung to view the wall where her chickens hung. Sure enough, Chloe's dust bath was missing. Marley blinked back emotion. Maybe it was just Gram's passing, or maybe it was more, but she'd been an emotional mess for the past week. At least since Alex's strange behavior the other night, like she suddenly repulsed him. He hadn't texted as often since.

Of course, neither had she. Rejection was natural, but she could mourn the loss of what had seemed a promising relationship. She should have known it wouldn't last, though. Nothing ever did.

Even her paintings deserted her to find new homes. She needed that to happen. They helped pay the bills and spread joy in the process, but each one was a part of her, just like the hens themselves.

Marley looked up at Wesley. "How do you deal with it? Those pieces you've spent hours and hours on — in your case, maybe days or weeks — and then they're gone?"

He blinked. "I'm not sure what you mean? What's to deal with?"

"Maybe men aren't as emotional. I feel like each piece is a part of me." She took a deep breath. "It's hard to say goodbye to them."

"Oh." Wesley scratched his neck. "I enjoy the creative process, for sure, but in the end, they're only products, only passing through my life. So, uh, yeah... not emotional."

"Come visit the hens," Kass said softly. "Maybe Wesley can give you some tips to help you with the letting-go process."

By the look the man gave his wife, Marley would bet he didn't know what they were talking about, but Kass seemed to get it. At least a little.

"Is tonight good?" asked Wesley. "Or you probably have a hot date with Alex."

If only. "He's putting in a lot of overtime these days, so I haven't seen much of him. Tonight would work for me."

Marley nearly missed the quick exchange of looks between the couple. What must it be like to know someone so deeply that a glance could become an entire private conversation?

Maybe someday she could experience that. If not with Alex, then with someone else. First, she needed to figure out a few things about her own life. Piece by piece, she was getting there.

⌒┈⌐

ALEX RUBBED HIS ACHING FOREHEAD. Only 7:00 pm. Unless he or one of the other guys had a massive break-through, they'd be here until ten. Again.

He pulled to his feet and headed to the break room for another coffee. He normally avoided caffeine in the evenings, but desperate times called for desperate measures and all that.

Sanderson's door was slightly ajar as Alex turned the corner of the corridor, and Nelson's plaintive voice drifted out. "Sir, it's really important. My wife—"

"How important is your job, Bristol? You nail down that

promotion, and that will make the little woman happy, won't it?"

What promotion? Alex stopped in his tracks and stared at the door with its embossed brass plate. The only upcoming promotion he knew of was his when the current VP retired. That's what Sanderson had been telling him, anyway.

"Yes, sir." But Nelson sounded tired. A chair squeaked from inside the room.

Alex ducked into the break room and reached for the coffeepot. The last bit in there was dank and tarry. Ugh. He dumped it in the sink and gave the carafe a swish under the faucet before filling it and exchanging the grounds for fresh ones. It would take a few minutes for a pourable cup, but he needed the break.

How his head hurt. He couldn't keep going like this much longer, but everyone on the floor was in his position, logging scraps of paper, sorting columns, trying to figure out what the deal was with this company their client wanted to purchase.

Sanderson could fire him if he refused the overtime. If he wanted to advance, he had to be a company man. Even Sanderson was in his office until the guys checked out at ten.

But was it Alex's promotion for the taking? He'd always thought so since his early days with the firm. But, Nelson...

Nelson Bristol stumbled into the break room, bloodshot and weary. "This is killing me."

"I hear you, man." Alex studied him while the coffee sputtered. "Sanderson's door was cracked open when I came by."

"Oh?" Nelson's gaze flicked from the coffeepot to Alex.

He tried to keep the edge out of his voice. Keep it casual. "What promotion are you up for?"

"VP, when Donaldson retires." Nelson shook his head. "It's supposed to be hush-hush, but since you overheard..." He reached for the carafe. "Think there's enough in there for a cup yet?"

Alex crossed the room and shut the door before turning to Nelson. No point making the same mistake and letting the boss overhear this conversation. "What would you think if I told you he promised the promotion to me?"

Nelson pivoted, his forehead furrowed in a frown. "Say what?"

Alex crossed his arms and waited.

"But that makes no sense. I've been here longer than you. Only a few months, but still. He's been grooming me since the beginning."

A sick feeling swirled in Alex's gut. "Ditto."

His coworker looked genuinely perplexed. "I don't get it."

"I wonder if he told Jovanic the same thing."

"What are you talking about, man?"

Alex glanced at the door, keeping his voice low. "Bristol, he's been priming me all along, too. Praising my progress, dropping hints of the corner office, and holding it up to lure me along." It was so clear now. The man had played to Alex's desire to succeed.

Carafe in hand, Nelson stared hard at Alex until coffee sputtered onto the element. Then he shoved the carafe back in place. "You're telling me we've both been had."

"I think so." Although *someone* would get the promotion. Alex rubbed the back of his neck. "Hush-hush here, too. 'It's our little secret for now.'"

"And a wink."

Oh, yeah. The wink.

Nelson slumped into the nearest chair. "What do we do now? I need this job."

"Me, too."

The door flew open, barely missing Alex. Their boss stormed in, his eyebrows raised as he looked between them. "Staff meeting and no one remembered to send me a memo?"

Alex pointed at the gurgling coffeepot. "It was out, so I made a fresh pot."

"Looks like enough there for a cup now. Back at 'er, Santoro. Bristol. I don't want to be here until midnight because you two are slacking off."

Nelson filled two mugs and stuffed the carafe back in place. "Want a cup, sir?"

"Nope. All I want is to see you hard at work."

Alex took his cup with the company logo on it and gave a mock salute with his other hand. "You've got it, sir." He strode from the room and down the hallway to his window-less cubicle. Settling into his chair, he loosened his necktie with his left hand while he nudged the mouse with his right.

The temptation to challenge his boss then and there had nearly overwhelmed him. Somehow, he'd bit back the angry words, and he needed to keep them under wraps until he'd had some sleep and come up with a plan of action.

Oh, yeah, and prayer.

He rubbed the back of his neck and stared at the screen. This was such a ridiculous project. He couldn't even imagine the number of billable hours for which the client was on the hook already... and they weren't done. Not by a long shot.

Was he doomed to this cubbyhole for decades? Clearly Sanderson had appealed to Alex's motivation for success. It stung. He'd been so gullible. Believed the man that he was a special snowflake, brighter and more deserving than anyone else.

Bristol had been told the same thing.

Two special snowflakes meant none, but Alex didn't need to ask Jovanic or anyone else if there were more of them. Two was enough to know he'd been had.

He'd stared so long his screen blinked to darkness.

No. Whatever he was going to do, it wasn't going to happen tonight. The rest of this week, at least, was all about keeping up appearances as a company man.

So he jiggled the mouse again and focused on the columns of numbers.

18

*M*arley dropped to her knees in Kass and Wesley's backyard and gathered her hens to her. Okay, not *hers* anymore. "Are you being a good girl?" She smoothed Ginger's feathers. "Giving lots of yummy eggs?"

"She does," Sebastian said earnestly. He sat beside her with Bianca on his lap.

Could chickens be traitors? Because they shouldn't love an eight-year-old boy as much as they loved her.

"Dad and I fixed their coop so it will be cozy for winter. See?" He pointed toward the workshop.

"It looks nice. I need to build one myself." Not that she had the skills, the time, or the cash. Huh. With the sales of the paintings, maybe she *could* afford it. It felt like blood money, but if it went to keep her hens happy, maybe it was a fair exchange.

"The d-days are getting shorter," Sebastian informed her. "We could get frost at night in September."

She smiled at the boy. "You're right. I'm running out of time. I'll figure something out really soon, okay?"

He nodded. "Good idea."

Marley gave Ginger one last rub and stood. "Where's your dad? I need to talk to him for a bit."

"He's bringing iced tea and cookies outside. Maybe I can have some, too."

Marley chuckled at the hopeful look. "You'll have to ask him or your mom, I guess." Oh, right. Kass wasn't the boy's mother.

"I will." He nodded and leaned closer. "Have you seen our baby? She's so cute, but s-sometimes she cries a lot."

"Babies are that way. Yes, I've seen her."

"I'm Mom's best helper."

How adorable was that? Obviously, the boy wasn't suffering with adjustments to his new family arrangements. "I'm sure you are."

The screen door opened and Wesley came out, carrying a tray. "Hey, Marley! Come on up here. You, too, Sebastian. Come have a couple of cookies then Mom needs you to help with Eleanor."

"Cool." The boy nudged Bianca off his lap then ran up the steps.

Marley followed more slowly, so Sebastian had already grabbed his treat and dashed inside before she took a seat at the glass patio table where a box of file folders and a closed laptop rested at one end. "Is this your summer office?"

Wesley chuckled. "Sure is. Of course, I have to take everything in and out, but that's a small price to pay for this view. Not only that, but I can drop a fishing line in the river on my coffee break if I want."

Marley hadn't thought about painting outdoors, but was there any real reason she couldn't? She didn't have the river at the foot of her yard, but she did have a rocky bluff at the back.

Oh, and an all-too curious neighbor in Kenji Ito. Never mind working outside until she had a taller barrier between their yards.

"So, tell me about your art background." Wesley passed her a tall glass of iced tea and settled into the chair across from her. "Oh, and have a cookie or two. Kass brought them home from the bistro. She tells me chewy chocolate peppermint cookies are one of the best sellers."

"They are." Marley took a sip. "Although nothing tops the sales of cinnamon rolls."

He chuckled. "I bet. Those things are amazing and addictive." He popped half a cookie in his mouth.

She took a deep breath. "I don't have any formal art training. It probably shows."

"Why would it show?" Wesley seemed genuinely perplexed.

"I'm sure there are things I could do better. This style just sort of... evolved from the bits I learned in high school art class and went from there."

"It's an original look. There's a lot to be said for that. How about business classes?"

She shook her head. "I didn't set out to create a business. In Yakima, I worked two jobs to make ends meet. I still wouldn't be thinking of selling paintings if Eden hadn't nudged me on that back in June."

"What were you going to do with them? Paper your walls?"

Marley felt a flush creep up her cheeks before she realized he was teasing her. "I hadn't thought that far," she admitted.

"I think you're telling me you haven't really studied business."

"You'd be right. I did save receipts the last couple of times I bought canvas and paints, though. And I have the sales reports from Kass." She stared at the table. "In a shoebox."

Wesley chuckled. "Don't let Alex hear you say that."

It probably wouldn't matter, anyway. Her heart caught, and she tried to keep her voice light. "I know, right?"

"You might want to sign up for a course or two at the college this fall, but meanwhile, let me show you the basics of a spreadsheet to keep track of things. I assume you have a computer?" He reached for his laptop.

"Yeah, but it's kind of old and runs slow. I do everything on my phone if I can." Which reminded her. "I have quite a few Instagram followers." Not that he'd be impressed. His art was so out of her league.

"Hey, that's cool. Kass is trying to get me on there, but it's always the last thing on my mind." He tapped a few keys on the laptop and then studied Marley. "I should ask... is it your goal to be a full-time artist? Because that makes a difference."

"Do you really think I could?"

"Possibly. It's a lot of work, and there are no guarantees, of course. But my advice will change depending on your answer."

"I never even thought of it, but I don't think so? I go stir-crazy by myself for too long. The chickens help some, but no matter how good my imagination, I can never carry on a satisfactory conversation with them for long."

Wesley tipped his head back and laughed. "I've tried to convince Bianca of a thing or two lately, and I agree. She doesn't care about my opinions."

A smile crept across Marley's face. She could hardly believe this accomplished sculptor and businessman was treating her as a peer.

Still grinning, he angled his laptop toward her. "Either way, you'll want to streamline everything you can. Here's what I suggest..."

⌒⌒⌒

"I'M STEALING HER." Ava hooked arms with Marley Sunday after church. "Since you didn't make plans."

Alex needed to make plans? He'd sat with Marley every Sunday for weeks and taken her to his parents' house for dinner. Today he'd been two minutes late at her door and she'd already left. When he arrived at church, she'd been wedged between Ava and Brittany in a full row, so Alex had sat further back. And now this?

Just because he'd had to work a ton of overtime this week? Or because he didn't know what to text her beyond, *I'm starting to hate my job*?

Marley flashed him a fleeting smile but didn't quite meet his eyes.

Irritation flashed through him. He might not have been the world's best boyfriend lately, but didn't a standing date count for anything? Couldn't she have told him she wanted to make other plans instead of making Ava spring it on him in a public place? Was Marley breaking up with him?

Alex was way too tired to think this through rationally. He hadn't been sleeping well since overhearing that conversation at work. His brain cells spent far too much of each night flapping around trying to figure out what to do next.

Maybe it was just as well Marley was busy with Ava. He wasn't likely to be good company anyway. Maybe he should excuse himself from family dinner and go for a long bike ride or something.

Marley turned away with Ava, and Alex suddenly realized he hadn't answered. See? His brain was a mess. He touched her shoulder. "Have fun. I'll talk to you later?"

"Okay." Again, her gaze didn't make direct contact.

He should be worried about this, but maybe it was for the best. Hadn't he been telling himself she wasn't his type? Alex rubbed his neck and bumped right into Jasmine as he turned.

His sister thumbed toward the retreating girls. "What was all that about?"

"I don't know." Alex tried to step around her. He was in no mood for her meddling.

"Want to talk?"

"Not really."

Jasmine grinned at him and thrust his niece into his arms. "Here, hold Lillian. She makes everything brighter."

He couldn't very well drop the baby, especially not when she gave him a wide toothless grin. He gave her a little bounce, and her smile widened. "Hey, baby girl. How old is she now, anyway?"

His sister rolled her eyes. "For a guy so good with numbers, I'd think you could keep track. Three months."

The smile he'd managed to find for the baby slipped away. Numbers. Sanderson was killing his love of them. "Jas, can you give Mom my apologies? I need some downtime today."

"Mr. Extrovert has had too much peopling? Hard to believe."

"It's true. Six twelve-to-fourteen-hour days at the office this week."

"Yikes. Peter told me you were putting in a lot of overtime, but that's more than a lot. That's insanity."

"Tell me." Alex glanced around the church foyer. Not many people remained. "Will you let Mom know?"

Jasmine shook her head. "I don't think so. You've got a phone. Tell her yourself." She leaned closer. "But I think you need some normal. Nonna's at Aunt Winnie's today, so she won't poke at you."

"Who needs Nonna when there's Nonna Junior?" He raised his eyebrows and gave Jasmine a pointed look.

"Me?" She laughed. "I'm an amateur compared to her. Come on, Alex. I'll even walk over with you so you can dump it all on me."

He looked around. "Where's Nathan?"

"He's over in Idaho this weekend, putting together a marketing package for the Green Acres Farm School."

"Oh." He let her tow him toward the door.

"You're not the only busy one, Alex. Granted, Nathan's not working an eighty-hour week, but the guys and I are pretty busy right now, too, with Bridgeview Backyards in full swing. I don't know what Peter and I will do without Landon and Jason. They're both headed into their Senior year. We'll have to find someone else to train come spring."

"How are you managing with the baby?"

"I keep Lillian with me when I can, and Nathan or Mom watches her when I can't. It's a bit of a juggle."

Alex looked at the wide-eyed baby in his arms as they

descended the church steps. "That will be harder when she can crawl or walk, won't it? I mean, not that I'm an expert."

"It will." Jasmine sighed. "You should come on board full-time, little brother. I can promise you fewer hours than you're putting in now. Also, less pay. What do you say?"

He chuckled. "You make it sound so appealing."

"Life isn't all about raking in big bucks, Alex. Slow down. Smell the roses."

"It's too seasonal. Too unpredictable."

"You're acquainted with our numbers. We're in our third season, and we're solid. We have clients on the wait-list, but we can't expand right now and take them on."

"Because of Basil."

"Yep. Buying him out was enough of a problem, but we've never been able to replace his manpower, either. Two teens part-time over the summer isn't the same as an invested partner."

Alex glanced at Jasmine. "You sound like you've forgiven him."

She shrugged. "More or less. You know me. I can hold a grudge with the best of them, but enough is enough. He's still an idiot, but keeping the anger burning was hurting me more than it was hurting him."

"You might be growing up."

"Ya think?" Jasmine slugged his arm. "Now, what's up with Marley?"

He shifted Lillian to his other arm. "Beats me if I know."

"Communication is not your thing?"

Alex glared at her. "You might not have noticed, but she and I are like polar opposites. I'm not sure how I thought we could ever work."

"What? You're crazy. She's the best thing that ever happened to you."

He'd thought so, too, but there'd always been that underlying thought that she was just too different.

"You do know that if you agreed on everything, one of you would be unnecessary?"

"What?" Alex stopped on the sidewalk.

"You heard me."

"No, I don't get it. Well, a bit. But don't couples need to have a lot in common? Though I doubt *you're* the expert, either."

"Some things, for sure." Jasmine shrugged. "But you're both believers. That's a good start."

"She's made some big strides in faith in the past few months."

"She really has. We talked about it the other day. She still has questions, but hey, don't we all?"

"You're hanging out with her?"

"Um, yeah? I've dropped by a few evenings this week to help her sort through Mrs. Renton's boxes. There's been a lot of junk but also some good stuff she can sell or repurpose."

Alex had been too hasty the other night. Judgmental, even, but man, her place had been a disaster. For a good reason, it turned out. He'd known that even then, but it was hard to get past. "Repurpose?"

"She's going to make kitchen curtains out of vintage tea towels. They'll be really cute."

He blinked.

"Marley has her own style, but it's very appealing." There was silence for a second. "Don't you think so?"

"Curtains out of old towels?" He tried to imagine. Failed.

"*Tea* towels," she corrected. "I'm borrowing Nonna's sewing machine one day soon and we'll do them up together. You'll see. They'll be adorable."

"See, that's the thing. What guy wants *adorable* kitchen curtains? I like my mini-blinds, thanks."

"Alex, with all due respect..."

A sentence that started with those words could hardly be respectful. Or pleasant. He raised his eyebrows at his sister.

"Your place is clinically clean. Sterile. Lifeless."

"I like it."

"Not everything has to be solid and functional. Loosen up a bit. Let the abstract in. The delicate, fragile glimpses of beauty. Have you ever stopped to admire cobwebs with dew on them?"

"I don't admire cobwebs in any form. Anywhere."

"That's what I mean. They're fragile, yet sturdy. Spun in a moment, yet with perfection. There's lots to appreciate when you open your eyes to fleeting bits of beauty. Glimpses of gossamer fill our lives with wonder."

19

*S*orry I'm late." Jasmine hurried into Marley's kitchen. "Lillian exploded right out of her diaper just as I walked out the door. She needed a bath, and we both needed a change of clothes."

It had been an awkward half hour with Marietta. First the old woman had examined Marley's yard and given her a hundred gardening tips, none of which Marley would remember.

She'd been so aware of the disheveled state back there. The herbs and flowers intermingled with what were probably weeds. Marley had pulled some she'd recognized for sure, like thistles, but she hadn't had time to keep up with it all lately. Not with working thirty hours a week, painting chickens to stay ahead of the amazing demand, and trying to reclaim the spare bedroom.

Seeing her poor excuse for a vegetable garden through Marietta's eyes had made her wince. A few tomato plants sprawled along the dirt, with the fruit pecked by the hens. Marley had salvaged some kale, and the spindly bean plants by Kenji's fence produced a meager return. Not at all what she'd hoped from this garden two months back.

Marietta looked up from the sewing machine. "Here. You teach Marley. I will take Lillian."

Jasmine winked at Marley as she unwrapped the baby sling. "She'd probably be happiest lying on her back kicking, though."

"I will hold her."

"There's a comfy chair in the living room," offered Marley. Comfy might be too strong a word, but the one she'd found in the spare room didn't have a broken spring like the old one.

Marietta plucked Lillian out of Jasmine's arms. The baby cooed and grinned. Her great-grandmother's face wreathed in the biggest smile Marley had yet seen as her tone changed completely. Baby talk in Italian got a happy response from Lillian.

Huh. The old woman might not be so bad after all. She truly seemed to love her family. That was good, right?

Jasmine leaned over the kitchen table. "How far did you get?"

"She showed me how to thread the machine."

"Okay, great. Have you decided which tea towels you want to use for this curtain?"

Marley laid out four. "I know they're not in order by days of the week, but that's how the colors look best to me."

Jasmine hesitated then nodded.

"Is that bad? Should I do it the other way?"

"No. No, it's fine."

Marley crossed her arms over her chest and lifted her chin slightly.

"Relax, girl. I was trying to see them through Alex's eyes."

"It's my kitchen, not his." Although she'd had some hope there for a few weeks.

"Alex is a stick-in-the-mud," announced Marietta. "He has no use for old things."

Marley blinked.

"We're all different," murmured Jasmine. "But maybe Alex is more different than most."

What was going on? Marley glanced between Marietta and Jasmine. "It's just..." Oh, whatever. She might as well jump all in. Both women no doubt already knew. "I haven't seen much of him for a couple of weeks, so I'm not sure why his opinion should matter. This is *my* home. My kitchen."

"Alex is a fool."

"Nonna," chided Jasmine.

"He is like a man old before his time. Focused on things long in the distance, when he should be looking at what is in front of his eyes." Marietta met Marley's gaze and gave a sharp nod.

"The tea towels?" asked Marley helplessly. "I just want pretty curtains out of them."

Marietta jiggled the baby and made a silly face. The baby chortled.

The tension in the room lifted slightly. Marley dared to breathe.

Jasmine fingered a tea towel. "You and Alex need to talk."

Marley shook her head. Wasn't that the guy's responsibility?

"And why not? Relationships go two ways. He's been

genuinely busy and stressed out at work. Plus, he's not a guy that easily talks about feelings. He's a numbers dude, and emotions aren't quantifiable."

Wasn't *that* the truth?

"My Salvador was the same," Marietta put in. "God rest his soul."

Marley had given little thought to the missing grandfather. She raised inquiring eyebrows at Jasmine.

"Nonni passed on when I was only four." Jasmine straightened and tossed her long braid over her shoulder. "I didn't know Alex was just like him, Nonna."

"He is a good man, Alessandro." Marietta eyed Marley. "A far-seeing man is better than one with no thought for tomorrow. And yet, sometimes such a one needs a reminder that life is to be lived moment by moment."

Jasmine chuckled. "I told him the other day to wake up and smell the roses."

"Exactly. But he may not be open to hear it from his sister or his nonna."

Or probably from Marley. Because it would sound too forward coming from someone like her with a somewhat dubious relationship between them. But, try as she might to ignore the fact that he was ignoring her, her thoughts went to Alex constantly. How was his day going? Was he getting enough rest? What was making him smile? Laugh?

He'd seemed so awkward Sunday. Maybe it had been wrong of Marley to put him to the test like that, agreeing to Ava's invitation. But if he truly loved her — not that they'd spoken *that* word — wouldn't he have protested rather than letting her go? But... had she given him a chance?

She had no idea how to do relationships. Not with the example her parents had offered. Not with the way her stepbrother had treated her. But, here in Bridgeview, she'd noted some good examples, like Alex's oldest brother, Marco, and his wife. Like Jasmine and Nathan. Or like Alex's parents.

They were all too good for her. She was still the girl from the wrong side of the tracks, with the garbage Brandon had pushed upon her. Reverend Smith had...

"Marley?"

She blinked back to the moment. Blinked back the tears. "Show me how to sew. Please." Her words came out a hoarse whisper.

Jasmine's arm circled her shoulder. "I'm sorry, sweetie. I shouldn't push you. I hate to see you hurting because of my stupid brother."

"It's not him." At least, not completely. "It's me. I'm not good enough."

"Nonsense," announced Marietta. "No one is good enough on their own. That's why Jesus came to save us."

Marley knew that. Grabbed onto it time and again until self-doubt ebbed away for a while. "How do you keep remembering?"

"Being in the Word daily. Asking God to keep your heart and mind fixed on Him."

Just like a couple of months ago when she'd asked Alex how he knew God was good. "Ask Him to show you," he'd said simply. "He will."

"There's a story in the Bible about Jesus' disciples being in a boat during a big storm," Jasmine put in. "Jesus walked toward them on the water, if you can imagine. Peter — the disciple, not my cousin — thought that would be cool, so Jesus invited him to come to Him. He did pretty well for a bit, and then he began to sink."

"I've read that story."

"You know what went wrong? He wasn't looking at Jesus. He started focusing on the size of the waves instead of his Savior. And his fear sank him."

The words pierced into Marley's heart. Was that what she was doing? Focusing on the wrong aspect of her life? "Pray for me?"

To Marley's surprise, Jasmine turned to her, placed both hands on her shoulders, and began to pray. Another hand pressed on her shoulder, and Marietta whispered, "Per favore."

Peace threaded through Marley's soul. Not just at the words in Jasmine's earnest prayer. Not just at the fervent agreement of Jasmine's nonna. But that someone cared so much for her that they would accompany her to Jesus.

She'd never forget this moment as long as she lived, right down to baby Lillian fussing as it went on.

"Amen," declared Marietta. "Now you sew. I must go home."

Marley blinked.

"If you wait a few minutes, I'll walk with you." Jasmine took the baby and laid her on the floor with a jingly toy at her feet.

"I am capable. I am not yet eighty years old."

"Not for a few weeks." Jasmine glanced at Marley. "I hope you're coming to the birthday party. It will be at the community center so there's room for all of Bridgeview to attend."

"I saw a notice on the bulletin board at the bistro."

"Alex didn't ask you? Well, *I'm* asking."

"Thank you." Marley smiled at Marietta, who stood with

her hand on the doorknob. "I'm sure it will be a great party."

"Humph." The door clicked shut behind Marietta.

"Really. You should come." Jasmine slipped onto the chair by the sewing machine. "Okay, see how I'm placing the two pieces of fabric with their backs together? I know that sounds wrong, but we're going to do a French seam so there won't be a raw edge showing. We'll sew a narrow seam on this side, then press it out and sew another from the other side to encase the narrow one. I'll show you."

A yelp came from out on the back step then a heavy crash.

Marley bolted for the door, Jasmine half a step behind her. Deirdre flapped away, squawking indignantly. Then Marley's gaze landed on Marietta crumpled over the wooden flower planter. "No!"

Jasmine dashed down the steps and knelt at her grandmother's side. "Nonna? Are you okay? What happened?"

The older woman made an effort to lift herself but moaned and fell back.

"Call 9-1-1," Jasmine ordered, smoothing the white hair away from Marietta's face. "She could have broken something."

With trembling fingers, Marley tapped the buttons.

⌖

ALEX'S CELL PHONE RANG, and he eyed it for a couple of seconds before reaching for it. Jasmine knew better than to phone him at work, so it must be an emergency. "Hey."

"Meet me up at the hospital. Nonna fell. The ambulance

just took her to Deaconess. Marley and I are following as soon as I get my car."

"Wait. What?" He rubbed his neck.

"Nonna." His sister's voice broke. "She passed out when they loaded her onto the stretcher. She must have broken some bones."

"Marley?"

"Oh. We were at Marley's house. Nonna tripped over one of her chickens, but we were inside and didn't see it happen. Kenji told us."

A shadow fell across Alex's desk, and he looked up to see his boss staring at him, eyebrows raised. Leaving the office right now could result in him not having a job. And what could he really do for Nonna? Nothing. That was up to the doctors.

"I can't come right now, Jas. Keep me updated, though."

"Alex, you have to—"

He tapped the End button and looked up at his boss. "My grandmother is headed to the hospital in an ambulance, sir."

"That's too bad. How old is she?"

"Nearly eighty."

Mr. Sanderson shook his head. "Good for her. At that age, you never know, right?"

That was it? A calloused reply. A flicker of ire began to rise in Alex. "That's not completely age-dependent. My uncle was only forty-seven when he died."

"Rough stuff." Mr. Sanderson rocked back on his heels. "How's that account coming along?"

Seriously? Slowly, Alex rose from his chair. "I need to go up to the hospital."

"For your grandmother? You have other relatives that can take care of things. You're needed here."

"My family needs me."

"Mr. Santoro."

Alex slipped his phone into his pocket and picked up his briefcase. "Yes, sir?"

"I wouldn't walk out of here if I were you."

"Mr. Sanderson, with all due respect, you aren't me. I have logged double time for two weeks, going above and beyond the call of duty, and right now, my family needs me. I'll see you in the morning."

"You can't—"

Alex brushed by his boss and passed Nelson Bristol's cubicle. His coworker gave him a wide-eyed questioning look, but Alex kept going. With the crazy long hours he'd been putting in, he'd started driving to work since he had no desire to bike home after dark, nor did he have the energy to do so. Today, he was thankful his car was in the parking garage next door.

He took the stairs rather than waiting for the elevator and, in a couple of minutes, headed south on Browne. It wasn't far to Deaconess. He parked and headed for the emergency entrance. It only took a moment to locate Marley, Jasmine, and Francesca huddled together.

"Alex!" Jasmine looked surprised to see him. "I didn't think you were coming."

"I'm here. What can I do?"

His cousin Fran grimaced. "Nothing. None of us can do anything. The doctors are back there examining her right now."

"Who's with her?" Surely someone was.

"Mom." Jasmine rubbed Lillian's back through the baby

wrap. "She swung by to get Marley and me on her way here since I'd walked over."

At last he let his gaze linger on Marley's tear-streaked face. Did she think so highly of Nonna? It was only a few weeks since she'd tried to avoid her. They'd made a game of it together.

Alex's heart tensed as he stepped closer. "You okay?"

Marley backed up and clenched her arms over her chest. "It's all my fault."

"It isn't." From Jasmine's expression, this wasn't the first time they'd had this talk. "It was an accident. It could have happened to anyone, anywhere."

"But it happened to your grandmother. At my house. Because I have free-range hens and—" she hiccupped "—a flower pot in the middle of nowhere."

Alex tried to piece it together. He turned to Jasmine. "What exactly happened?"

"Kenji said Nonna turned to say something to him, tripped over a chicken, and fell across the planter."

He looked at Marley. "Is he still watching you all the time?"

She hiccupped again. "He doesn't bother me much. Not really."

Why was she downplaying it? Alex was going to have a talk with him. It wasn't right. It was... creepy.

A nurse approached. "Family of Marietta Santoro?"

20

*M*arley didn't want to hear what the nurse had to say. All she could see was Marietta sprawled over that stupid planter at an awkward angle. Broken. Unmoving.

She couldn't stay in Bridgeview if coming to her place had killed Alex and Jasmine's grandmother. But she owned the house, so it wouldn't be as easy to move on as it used to be. What was she supposed to do? How could she live with herself?

Why was she even at the hospital with the family? She'd been caught up with Jasmine when she called her mother. Before she knew it, she was in Grace's car, and Jasmine was buckling Lillian into the baby seat her mom kept in the trunk.

Alex and Jasmine and their cousin Fran asked questions of the nurse in low tones, their backs to Marley. She wasn't part of this family. She never would be. This would be a good time to leave. There was a taxi stand outside, but she'd left her backpack purse at home. Still, it wasn't far to Bridgeview. She could walk it in probably half an hour.

Marley sidled toward the sliding glass doors, but they whooshed open before she got there. Two paramedics with a gurney between them strode through. A teen girl lay on the white sheet, tangled blond hair fanned out and framing a bruised, bloody face.

No! Marley's hand covered her mouth as she stared after them. Deaconess's emergency room distorted into Allenmore's in Tacoma. The girl morphed into Marley. The antiseptic hospital smells sharpened. Fear curdled in her stomach.

It had been just an accident, Brandon assured her. Assured their father, the police officer, and the emergency doctor. He'd been angry, yes, but she'd startled him, stepped in his way. The target had been the post beside her. He would never hurt her.

Had she really stepped into his path? Why hadn't she run? She'd perfected evading him for two years. His knowing looks. His marginally inappropriate touches. Brandon had never crossed the line with something she could take to Dad. His temper flashed hot, but he'd never been violent. He was too good for that. Too careful.

So his story made sense.

Kind of.

But she'd had nightmares for weeks of him leaning closer, his breath hot on her cheek. *It won't be an accident next time.* Just her imagination, or had he whispered those words?

Marley was through the glass doors before they slid shut. She darted down the sidewalk, her breathing heavy, needing to get away from Brandon. But it wasn't Brandon.

Think, Marley. That was five years ago. Dad died of an over-dose. You escaped to Yakima. Then to Spokane. Brandon isn't here.

What was she running from then?

Alex. She wasn't good enough for him. He embodied everything she couldn't have in life. Brandon was gone, but he'd been right about some things. She'd never be anything but a girl with a messy past. Reverend Smith's face joined Brandon's, shaking his head accusingly at what Marley had become.

She ran through the I-90 underpass and turned west on Third before she took a breath. This was a one-way. Alex couldn't follow here. But why would he? She'd barely seen him for two weeks. He'd already figured out what a loser she was. Now the rest of his family knew it, too.

To think she might be responsible for Alex's grandmother's death. The weight would crush her. She'd have no choice but to sell out and leave Bridgeview. She'd start over somewhere else.

Gasping sobs surged from her gut, nearly doubling her over. Tears coursed down her cheeks. Seeing a bench along the sidewalk, she dropped into it, holding her face in her hands.

Jasmine's words penetrated her swirling mind. *You know what went wrong? Peter wasn't looking at Jesus. He started focusing on the size of the waves instead of his Savior. And his fear sank him.*

Had that only been an hour or two ago? Marley had felt the deepest peace of her life, but it hadn't lasted.

But God was a good, good Father. What had Pastor Tomas said? God was unchangeable. He wasn't going to love Marley one minute and mock her the next. Pastor Tomas had been preaching a series on the qualities of God over the past couple of months. God was good. He was wise. He was loving. Faithful. Merciful.

Marley flicked on her phone to that YouTube video Alex had shown her and let *Good, Good Father* play through twice.

She hadn't had a good father. Dad had dabbled in drugs for years. He'd struggled to keep a decent job or a decent woman. He'd cared for her in his own way, but wasn't really capable of love. Not the kind of love Marley had seen in her neighbors.

In Jesus.

Peter had taken his eyes off Jesus and sank into the tumultuous sea. Right where Marley was now. Sinking... for the same reason.

"Jesus?" she whispered. "It's me, Marley. I'm sorry. I've messed up again. I don't want fear to sink me any longer. I believe in the God at Bridgeview Bible Church. The God Pastor Tomas preaches about. Whom Alex loves. I've asked You before to come into my life but then kept doing my own thing. Please, please forgive me. Help me."

Soft, downy peace began to settle the churning in her gut.

"And please be with Alex's nonna. Don't let her die." Marley wiped her damp cheeks. Should she ask about Alex, too? No. That was selfish. She didn't deserve—

Wait. Who said anything about deserving love?

"God? One more thing. It's about Alex—"

Her cell phone rang. Her eyes sprang open, but it was Jasmine. Marley hesitated a second. *No fear. You gave it to God, remember? Step out into the waves.* "Hi?"

"Marley! Where are you? We've been looking all over for you."

"I'm sorry. I-I needed some air. Hospitals bring back

bad memories." *One more thing, God. About that girl on the stretcher. Could You heal her?* She braced herself. "How's your grandmother?"

"They're admitting her. She broke several ribs and has two hairline fractures on her pelvis. Oh, and her arm, but at least they can cast that."

Guilt swarmed Marley. *Eyes on Jesus. Eyes on Jesus.* "Will she be... okay?"

"They think so. Just she's pretty much immobilized for now. Don't worry, Marley. It wasn't your fault."

"But it was."

"Not even a little bit."

"But—"

"She doesn't blame you. Neither do I. It was an accident. She wasn't looking where she was going when she turned. It was a comedy of errors."

"Comedies are supposed to be funny."

"It's just a turn of phrase. Seriously, though, where *are* you?"

"Walking home. I'm fine. In fact, I'm nearly there. You stay with your grandmother as long as you need to."

"If you're sure?"

"Definitely." Marley tapped to end the call and stared at the busy traffic. Jasmine hadn't said anything about Alex. But Marley could still hold onto Jesus' love.

⌒◡

Dude, Sanderson is on a rampage.

Alex stared at Nelson's text and chewed his lip. The busy ER whirled around him. The acrid stench of something like fear mixed with blood and antiseptics assaulted his nostrils.

Nurses and paramedics spoke calmly and firmly into the sterile silence, punctuated by a woman's sobs across the waiting room.

He looked at his phone again. There wasn't anything he could do for Nonna, just like Sanderson had said. Mom was still back there with her, while Jasmine had settled into a corner to feed Lillian. An ever-expanding group of family members gathered around Fran, who was more than capable of dispensing information and recruiting volunteers, not that Alex had any idea what anyone could do. His aunts had gathered. Daria and Marco. Brittany. Ava. Peter.

Part of Alex was angry enough — stubborn enough — to leave Sanderson fuming for a while longer, but he just couldn't do it. His sense of responsibility and, yes, control, was too great. If he left the firm, it would be on his own terms, not from obstinacy. Unless it already was too late, in which case he'd survive.

He crossed to where Jasmine sat and dropped into the chair next to her. "Sanderson's in a rage. I need to get back to the office."

His sister looked over at him. "I don't know why you put up with him."

"Says the gal who could never stomach working for anyone else." She'd had her own massage therapy practice before starting Bridgeview Backyards with Peter and Basil.

"Guilty as charged. There's pros and cons, of course."

"I know. I live with Peter."

Jasmine slipped Lillian out from under the cover and began patting her back. "Aren't you going to ask about Marley?"

Alex sucked in a sharp breath and looked around the waiting area. "Where is she?"

"She left in a panic. Something about hospitals triggering bad memories." Jasmine eyed him. "She's convinced Nonna's accident is her fault."

She'd said the same to Alex. "I can kind of see her point…"

"Alexander!"

Whoa. He blinked. "All I meant is it happened at her house. Over her chicken. Over her planter. So I get why she feels that way."

"It could have happened anywhere. Sure, that's what Nonna tripped *over*. But that doesn't mean fingers need to be pointed and accusations made."

Alex opened his mouth and closed it again. But he couldn't hold it back. "Accusations? I'm not blaming her for anything. Other than you have to admit her place is pretty messy. There's plenty to trip over."

"I thought you and Marley were dating. Maybe falling in love."

"It's complicated."

Jasmine rolled her eyes. "Isn't it always? But why do you have to make it more difficult than it needs to be? She's the perfect antidote to you."

"Because I'm a poison?" He couldn't keep the sarcasm out of his voice. "Thanks, Jasmine."

"That's not what I meant. Here, hold the baby." She thrust Lillian at him and adjusted her clothing.

Alex averted his gaze and lifted the baby overhead, jiggling her and babbling nonsense as she grinned in all her toothless wonder.

"I wouldn't—"

A blurp of milk erupted from Lillian's mouth and

cascaded down Alex's gray shirt and favorite navy silk tie. "Ugh!"

"Man, Alex. This isn't your first rodeo. I thought you knew better." Jasmine dragged a cloth out of her backpack and dabbed at his shirt.

"Like that's going to work." He pushed the baby into his sister's lap. "I need to go home and change. And I need to get back to the office before I get fired."

Jasmine grabbed his arm as he rose. "Alex? What are you going to do about Marley?"

He ground his teeth. "I don't know, snoopy sister. I think we're just too different."

"You're full of yourself."

"Excuse me?"

"You're saying 'my way or the highway.' That's not how love works, little brother. God made us different for a reason, and I'm not just talking about biology. I'm talking about each partner bringing strengths to the table that the other one doesn't have. Even you are not strong in every area, Alex. I'm not sure what you feel you need to prove. It's like you're trying to be this paragon. What drives you?"

What was it with Jasmine? She could flick a blade under his ribs quicker than just about anyone, long before he could see it coming.

She stood, swinging Lillian to her hip. "If you're trying to be 'not Basil,' you already have that covered. You don't have to prove anything in this family, Alex. God made you to be *you*. You're a good you."

He stared at her, mind whirling with all the events of the morning. Finally, he said, "I really need to go, Jasmine. Keep me updated on Nonna."

"You've got it. And, Alex?" She rested her hand on his forearm as he turned away.

"Yeah?"

"I'm praying for you. I think there's stuff going on you need to deal with before you can make things work with Marley. You're not ready."

"Stop meddling."

Jasmine flashed him a grin. "You need me."

"I don't think so. Gotta go."

Alex strode out the sliding glass doors and down the sidewalk toward his car. He hated like the dickens thinking Jasmine was right about anything at all, but she had made a couple of good points in there.

He needed to wrap his brain around his feelings for Marley. Ignoring them wasn't working. Avoiding her wasn't working. She still danced in his dreams. Could he accept her as she was? That, like Jasmine had reasoned, Marley was the best version of herself she could be? No, not perfect. No one was. Definitely not Alex... but was it wrong to try? God didn't want him to be satisfied with his imperfections, did He?

Okay, yes, he had some unresolved issues with Basil. His brother had messed with Alex's psyche from their childhood on. Was that why Alex felt so driven to succeed? So people would see which brother was the solid, responsible one?

His job. His brother. His walk with God. Marley.

For a guy who'd thought he had it all together, he had some work to do. If only every change were as simple as switching out his shirt and tie for a clean one.

21

*I*t had been a week since Marietta's fall and hospitalization, and Marley had yet to see Alex. Not that she was looking for him, exactly. She'd skipped church to avoid him as that was the most likely place. Longest Sunday ever.

Jasmine had come by to help finish the tea towel curtains then taken Marietta's sewing machine with her. They hadn't spoken of Alex.

Marley worked her regular hours at the bistro. Painted more chickens, since they seemed to keep selling. Sorted the last of Gram Renton's boxes and waved goodbye to the thrift store truck hauling the usable items away. Ordered a small wooden coop from a farm supply store.

She sat on her back steps in the gathering dusk, her hens nestled around her, Deirdre in her lap. The Cochin seemed none the worse for wear after causing Marietta's accident. Marley stroked her soft black-and-white feathers, and Deirdre leaned into the touch. For once, Kenji wasn't in his yard that she could see.

Traffic rumbled by on the bridge accompanied by an occasional siren. The fragrance of the herbs and flowers wrapped around Marley, adding to her cocoon.

Marley looked up at the few stars visible in the darkening sky. God was so awesome. So amazing. She'd been reading The Voice version of the Bible lately, and some of the verses came back to mind. She hated the glare of her phone display in the dark, but needed to reread the familiar words from the eighth Psalm.

I can't help but wonder why You care about mortals — sons and daughters of men — specks of dust floating about the cosmos. But You placed the son of man just beneath God and honored him like royalty, crowning him with glory and honor. You ordained him to govern the works of Your hands, to nurture the offspring of Your divine imagination; You placed everything on earth beneath his feet.

Flecks of dust floating in the cosmos. That was about the size she felt. The importance. And yet... the psalmist went on to show the value the Creator placed on his creation. And in that other Psalm... where was it again? She tapped a phrase into search. Ah, Psalm 91.

He who takes refuge in the shelter of the Most High will be safe in the shadow of the Almighty. He will say to the Eternal, "My shelter, my mighty fortress, my God, I place all my trust in You." For He will rescue you from the snares set by your enemies who entrap you and from deadly plagues. Like a bird protecting its young, God will cover you with His feathers, will protect you under His great wings; His faithfulness will form a shield around you, a rock-solid wall to protect you.

Marley had placed all her trust in the Eternal. Looking back, it had been He who'd rescued her from Brandon, from her past. And watching her chickens fluff out their feathers as they settled to the ground gave her the visual of being protected by God's feathers. He'd definitely shielded her.

So what if she and Alex drifted apart, and he eventually married someone else? She'd just have to accept that if it happened. God had brought her to Bridgeview and given her this little house, complete with the rock-solid wall angling up in her backyard to remind her of His faithful shield. She wasn't going anywhere.

Crickets chirped. Deirdre shifted, murmuring sleepily. Next door, a car engine cut out then a door shut. The motion-sensor kicked a light on, and she glanced over to see Alex mounting his back steps wearing shorts and a T-shirt. He wasn't coming from the office, then. Was the urgent rush at work over? But where had he been?

A little part of her shriveled inside. She'd been telling herself it was all because of his job. That he wasn't really avoiding her, just super busy and stressed. He'd *sounded* stressed in the emergency room last week.

He went into his house, and the light flicked out.

"God?" Marley looked up at the night sky again, this time wiping a few tears from her cheeks. "I really wanted this to work with Alex."

Why did she have to be the one who waited? Why couldn't she be the one to try to repair the rift between them? But she hadn't caused the problem, had she? When had it all started? With his long hours. Maybe she'd been less than understanding. Applied pressure. But she hadn't.

No, she couldn't march over there and try to get to the bottom of it. Whatever was going on was inside him. She couldn't help.

But Jesus could.

"I NEED to take tomorrow off work, sir."

Mr. Sanderson steepled his hands on his desk and looked at Alex from beneath raised eyebrows. "I don't hear a question in there, Santoro."

"There isn't one, sir. I know we're caught up at the office, and my family has called a work day to get my grandmother's house ready for her discharge from rehab."

"They're putting you in charge of a dust cloth?"

Alex widened his stance, hands behind his back. "Possibly. Or an electric screwdriver. It doesn't much matter to me."

"Listen, Santoro. Why don't you have a seat?"

"No, thank you."

"Suit yourself. Let me explain how things work in this firm." He lowered his voice. "Although I thought you clearly understood that promotions come to team players."

"You've made that clear, yes."

"And you've seen the view from Mr. Donaldson's office."

"Yes, sir."

A rustle came from behind him. "As have I, sir."

Alex turned slightly as Nelson nudged the door open and stood beside him. They nodded at each other.

"Well, isn't this interesting." Mr. Sanderson leaned back in his chair and looked between them.

Alex set a legal-size envelope on the desk. "My two-weeks' notice, sir."

"Mine as well." Nelson laid his on top. "Sir."

The chair flew back against the window as Sanderson surged to his feet. "Now listen here. You can't just up and quit. Either of you. There's work to be done."

"And you receive a handful of qualified applications daily, as you've mentioned." Alex regarded him steadily. "I'm sure you'll have no problem replacing us both."

"In two weeks! You can't do this."

"But we are." Nelson parked his hands on his hips. "And I have a word of advice for you."

"Get out."

"Don't play your employees against each other, sir. That's all I've got to say." Nelson pivoted on his heel and strode out.

Sanderson narrowed his gaze at Alex, fury emanating from every pore of his body. "What do you think you're doing?"

"Taking control of my own destiny. Or, rather, letting God take control instead of my ego."

"God." The man's eyes rolled. "What's He got to do with anything?"

"More than you'd think. You nurtured a belief I was really somebody. My life was all planned out in the what's-best-for-Alex kind of way. And what was best for Alex was clearly VP and, yes, that corner office you dangled in front of me. In front of Nelson, too."

Sanderson's jaw tensed, but Alex charged on.

"I don't need a corner office, but I would like one with a view. Oh, walls and a door would really help me focus, too. So Nelson and I are hanging out our own shingle. Our new location has a great view of the river."

Sanderson placed both hands on his desk and leaned in. "Don't you dare steal any of my clients."

"You have my word we won't go after a single one of them, but we won't turn them away if they come knocking, either. Although we have several accounts lined up already.

Clients who are looking for a more personal touch than a big company like yours can offer."

"You're really doing this." Sanderson tapped the envelopes. "I can't believe you're shafting the man who trained you. You'd be nothing without me."

"The training has been invaluable, sir. Thank you for the opportunity. I'll see you Thursday, and I'll work hard every single weekday until the end of August." Alex nodded firmly. "Good day, sir."

He strode out of the office and nearly mowed Nelson over.

"You're a better man than I am, Santoro. I was about to lose my cool. Figured I'd better get out of there before I blew it."

Alex shook his head. "He does get to a guy. See you Thursday."

"And Saturday." Nelson fell into step beside him as they headed back to the semi-open office area. "Can't wait to get rid of the vibrant pink walls in our new place."

They'd rented a small space in a business building down near Bridgeview. Alex grinned. "They're certainly cheerier than all the gray around here."

"You can keep the pink in your office. Wait, no, you can't. I'll have to come in for consultation at times, and I don't think I could handle it."

"I was thinking of peach."

Nelson slugged his arm. "You nearly had me."

"One wall in something darker, like rust. With a few pieces of whimsical art on it. I've been thinking chickens." If Marley would sell him any after all he'd put her through.

"I... I'm not sure what to say, man."

"Make your office your own, Bristol." Alex locked his

fingers together and stretched his hands over his head. "No. More. Gray. We've got a new lease on life."

"I might be jealous." Clint Jovanic leaned out of his cubicle. "You guys are really doing this? Sandy would kill me if I quit here."

"Maybe *you'll* get the VP promotion." Nelson punched Clint's shoulder. "Maybe the big boss has learned something over the past couple of weeks."

Clint sighed. "One can hope."

"Well, I'm out of here." Alex rocked back on his heels. "Taking tomorrow off, so I'll see you Thursday." He grabbed his briefcase from his cubicle next to Clint's.

"Taking a day off... is that really a thing?" Clint's plaintive voice followed Alex out of the office.

Yes. In Alex's new world, it was.

⌒ᴗᴖ

MARLEY WALKED up the street after work. She'd seen Alex's dad and uncles building a wheelchair ramp out front of Marietta's house when she'd headed down the hill earlier. Ava told her the family had gathered together to scrub the house top to bottom, rearrange furniture to facilitate a wheelchair, and install grab bars in the master bathroom. They'd even hired a nurse to live-in during Marietta's convalescence.

Once Marley had dreamed she'd become part of this family, but that thought had faded slightly with each day that Alex didn't show his face. She hadn't asked Jasmine or Ava any leading questions. Her heartache was none of their business. Marley needed friends more than she needed to be passionately loved.

Maybe someday when her heart had recovered a bit, she'd confront Alex so she'd know how to avoid a falling out like this next time. Next time what? Next time she fell in love? Not happening. And with that thought, she knew she couldn't talk to him yet. She was way too raw.

Her steps slowed. A van was pulled up to the ramp, and Marietta's front door stood wide open. She could march in there and welcome the old woman home. See with her own eyes that tripping over Deirdre hadn't caused any permanent damage. But it was after five, and Alex might be inside now that he apparently wasn't working until dark every night.

No, she'd keep going. Two more paintings had sold from the bistro, and she had nothing finished to replace them with. Maybe once Kass returned, Marley could work fewer hours and keep up better. She definitely didn't want to quit, though. The buzz around the corner café was too invigorating.

Jasmine flew out of the front door and down the ramp. "Marley! Won't you come in for a minute?"

"I don't think so. Maybe another time. I'm sure your grandmother is tired from everything going on around her."

"Probably, but I know she'll want to see you." Jasmine tugged at her arm.

Marley shook her head, but a movement from the house caught her eye. Alex stood framed in the doorway. Marley pulled away from Jasmine. "I need to go." She had only taken half a dozen steps when she felt his presence. Smelled his favorite cologne, which just so happened to be hers, too.

"Marley? Can we talk?"

Why now? But she wouldn't shut him out like he'd shut

her. "Um, sure?" Oh, man. Her voice totally came out breathless.

"I've been a jerk, and I'm sorry."

Well, that was blunt. She snuck a peek at him. Both hands were wedged in his shorts pockets, his gaze fixed up the street.

She could do frank, too. "Yeah, you were."

"There's been a lot going on, but that's no excuse. I got scared. Pushed you away. You didn't deserve that."

"What did I do wrong?" Marley managed to keep her voice solid, but her hands twitched with the desire to smooth his hair, disheveled for the first time since she'd met him. To trace his cheeks with her thumbs. To lean in and—

Nope.

Alex glanced her way and caught her looking. He stopped on the sidewalk and turned to her. Their gazes tangled. His hands found hers and gripped tightly. "It's not you, Marley. It's me." His voice was husky.

"I'm not sure what you mean." The man was practically perfect.

"I... this is hard." He took a deep breath. "I'm a neat freak kind of guy. I like everything in its place. I—"

Marley pulled her hands out of his. "And I'm not that way. I get it." She took a few steps up the sidewalk before she caught a glimpse of him beside her from the corner of her eye.

"God's been talking to me about that."

Say what? She looked over, eyebrows raised.

"Not only a neat freak but a control freak." Alex bit his lip, but his gaze met hers. "And controlling things isn't my job. It's God's. I don't like leaving things to Him or, for that matter, to anyone else."

Whereas Marley had grown up wishing she could control something. Anything. But it all seemed out of reach. Why even try?

"Marley? I let my issues come between us instead of accepting you how you are. I felt you should be this flawless woman of my dreams."

Marley shook her head and backed up a step. For a few seconds she'd had a glimmer of hope once again, but it was not to be. "I'm not perfectly anything except maybe a mess. If that's what you're looking for, have a nice life."

"I'm not looking for perfection. Not anymore." Alex reached for her hands.

What was he saying? Could she read the real meaning in his eyes? Because his words made no sense.

He grimaced. "Even that came out wrong. You may not be perfect, but neither am I. Mainly, though, you're perfect for me. You have strengths where I have weaknesses. I have strengths where you do. It took me a while to see the value of that, but now... all I can do is beg your forgiveness for my arrogance and stupidity. I love you, Marley. I hope you'll forgive me. Give us another chance."

The words hung in the air between them. He loved her? But what was love? More than a mushy feeling. Love was a commitment to admitting failure. To asking forgiveness. To listening to each other. Actually hearing.

She could test that right now. "I'm afraid of love."

Alex squeezed her fingers gently. "Why?"

"Because I've never seen it up close. Because I don't know how to do it."

"I don't know how, either. But can we learn together?"

"We can try," Marley whispered. She freed her hands so she could rest them on his hips, and her whole body thrilled when he tugged her closer. "Maybe we can learn how to love from God's word."

"Let's study together. Like First Corinthians chapter thirteen." His hands stroked her back.

"I'd like that." She could get no air, he was so close. "Are we... really okay?"

He dipped his head and caressed her lips with his own.

A whoop went up from his grandmother's house down the street.

Heat flashed up Marley's neck and across her cheeks. What must Alex's relatives think?

"We seem to have an audience." Alex gave her a lopsided grin. "Want to give them something to talk about?"

22

*W*ow, there are a lot of people here!" Marley turned in amazement, taking in the crowd in the community center, dragging Alex around with her, since their fingers were entwined.

Alex bumped her shoulder with his own. "And I'm not even related to all of them."

Nearly, though. Over the three months she'd lived in Bridgeview, she'd met most of Alex's aunts, uncles, and cousins, even the ones who lived out of the city. Every one of them had come out of the woodwork for Marietta's 80th birthday party today.

"Marley, I'd like you to meet my brother Basil."

Marley turned to see a taller version of Alex. Not quite as good looking, of course, but she could see the family resemblance. "Hello, Basil. I'm pleased to meet you at last."

Alex's brother raised one eyebrow as he looked her up and down. "The pleasure is all mine. I've heard a lot about you from multiple sources." He gave Alex a measuring look. "But not a lot from my little brother."

Alex grinned. "I've been kind of busy getting a new business started and all. And in between, I've been working for Peter and Jasmine. You should move back, Basil. They really need a permanent hand."

His brother rolled his eyes. "Being a Santoro in Bridgeview is not my idea of a good time." He nodded at Marley. "Poor you. Stick around my brother, and you'll be saddled with the infamous surname."

A flush crept up Marley's cheeks. She and Alex had been dating again for a few weeks, but they'd skirted the subject of their future over and over again. Although, she'd secretly practiced signing her name Marley Santoro... and kind of liked the flourish she placed on the end.

"Hey, now. It's not that bad." Alex waved around the crowded community center. "Even though our nonna has a sharp tongue, everyone in Bridgeview loves her. It took me a while to figure out, but you don't have to be perfect to be a Santoro."

"Easy for you to say, golden boy." Basil's upper lip curled slightly. "Some of us do better from a distance. It's not just me who needed to escape." He nodded toward a family that had just come in the double doors. Marley had seen their portrait on Marietta's wall. She couldn't wait to meet them. Enough of his older brother's toxicity. She tugged at Alex's hand.

"Well, I'm sure you have a lot of people to catch up with around here." Alex seemed to catch her drift. "People are practically standing in line to talk to you. There's Jacob and Eden and their newborn twins. You'll want to see them."

Oh, so did Marley! The babies were only a week or so old, two little girls they'd named Anya and Indigo for Eden's sisters. But this wasn't her moment.

Alex pulled Marley toward the newcomers. "Hey, Rob! Good to see you, man. And you, too, Bren." He ruffled their daughter's hair and punched the older boy's arm. The toddler in Rob's arms tucked his head against his daddy's neck and smiled shyly.

"You must be Marley." Rob stretched his free hand for hers, but her fingers were tangled up in Alex's. She managed to get them loose as Rob's wide grin erupted into chuckles. Then he looked at Alex. "Good to see you, Alex. And congratulations on starting your own business. I'm sure that will keep you occupied and out of trouble." His gaze drifted to Marley with a grin. "Or possibly not."

Alex laughed while he and his cousin exchanged man-hugs complete with back-slapping. "We really need to make opportunities for a clan gathering a little more often."

"We'll be back for Peter and Sadie's wedding at Thanksgiving," Bren said. "And then again at Christmas. Rob's parents can't get enough of spoiling the kids."

"Things going well for you in Helena? Still working for Todd O'Brien's marketing agency?"

The other man nodded. "Sure am. Not all of us have that entrepreneurial bent like you do, Alex."

Marley felt like her buttons would pop with the pride she felt in her boyfriend.

Alex shook his head with a grin. "I never thought I had it, either. But it's nothing compared to Marley. Have you seen her artwork?"

Bren turned a smile toward Marley. "I follow you on Instagram. I sure hope we can pick up a painting or two while we're here this weekend."

Marley managed a smile, but it still seemed crazy how many people loved her art. Wesley had shown her how to make prints and now she was able to increase her sales by adding a lower-priced product. He had also talked her into asking more for the original paintings.

Bren and Rob's daughter, Lila, pulled away from her mom. "There's Tieri!" And off she ran.

"Michael should be around here somewhere, Davy," Rob said to his son. "If you boys decide to go over to the basketball court, let your mom or me know."

"So how are things with Bridgeview Backyards?" Rob asked as his son ambled away. "Bren and I are talking about shifting Hiller Farm in that direction rather than continuing on as part of Tomah CSA. We're still committed for the coming growing season, and we've got lots of research to do before we make a change. If we do."

"You're best off talking to Peter or Jasmine about that," Alex said. "I'm only helping out these days because they're so desperate for extra hands. Nelson and I have plenty enough business at the new office to keep going."

Bren turned to Marley. "Seriously, girl. I don't know how you do it all. You are my new hero."

Wasn't that a breath of fresh air after Basil? Marley smiled at Alex's cousin's wife. "It's not that amazing, really. I only work thirty hours a week at the bistro, and my yard and chickens don't take up that much time. The rest of it, I spend painting."

Rob nudged Alex. "When do you see her?"

Alex grinned at Marley. She'd never get tired of the way his eyes lit up when he looked at her. "I never knew how fun it would be to watch someone paint. Sometimes I even read to her while she works. And other times, she comes with me and picks vegetables for the family business."

He failed to mention that he'd mostly taken over

keeping her kitchen clean to give her more painting time. Things had sure changed in the past few weeks.

"You live right next door, don't you?" Bren asked. "Where are you guys going to live when you get married?"

Marley flushed, feeling the heat erupt across her face. The question had been poking her, too, but it wasn't something they'd discussed. She didn't dare look at Alex.

Rob laughed and slid his arm around his wife. "I think you're jumping the gun on them, sweetheart. Give them a bit more time to figure things out."

Part of Marley remembered she and Alex had only known each other three months, but part of her felt like she'd lived in Bridgeview forever, that she and Alex had been destined from birth to be soulmates. She continually cautioned her love-struck self to be patient and enjoy the season she was in. But wouldn't a special day like today be a great day to make things more permanent? She had no doubt what her answer would be... a resounding yes.

⁓ ℓ ℭ

THE ONLY THING better than a Santoro clan gathering was one that included all of Bridgeview. Alex tucked Marley tight against his side and surveyed the noisy crowd. Tony's parents, Uncle Matteo and Aunt Connie, were down from Galena Landing, Idaho, for the weekend, as well as his sister Gina's family. With Rob's family here from Montana, and Basil and Dominic home from Seattle, the Santoros were complete.

Except for Uncle Al.

Alex looked for Aunt Winnie, but she was smiling up at her eldest son. She'd done so well since Al passed away two years ago. If there was a crack in her armor, Alex hadn't heard anyone mention it. How would he handle it if something happened to Marley prematurely? And they weren't even engaged, let alone married.

Didn't mean Alex wasn't thinking about it. While he wasn't planning to wait for his thirtieth birthday as he'd once — foolishly — thought, he still knew it was better not to rush. He and Marley had the rest of their lives to spend together.

"Kenji," breathed Marley, twisting toward the door.

Alex turned with her to see the elderly man step into the community center, framed by the sunlight outside. This was a first. Had Kenji Ito attended a single neighborhood gathering since they'd opened the renovated building three years back? Not that Alex could remember.

The chatter dimmed as Kenji took a few steps inside. Curious gazes turned his way.

Marley tugged Alex's hand as she headed toward her neighbor. "Mr. Ito, it's good to see you."

Kenji dipped his head toward her, but turned his gaze back to Nonna.

"You're here to see the birthday girl! Well, come with me."

And she let right go of Alex and tucked her hand behind Kenji's elbow. She chatted at him as she led him toward Nonna.

Alex stood staring, pretty sure he had a stupid grin across his face. Wasn't Marley amazing? She'd come such a long way in three months. But his place was at her side, so he hurried to catch up.

Voices picked up as people resumed their visiting.

"Marietta! Look who's come to wish you a happy birthday."

Nonna turned gingerly in her wheelchair and held out one hand. "Kenji. You came."

The old man bowed over her hand and kissed it.

Alex's eyebrows shot up. What on earth? Marley cast him a wide-eyed look.

"Are you well, Marietta?"

"I will be. And you?"

"Good, good." Then Kenji seemed aware of their audience. He dropped Nonna's hand and took a step backward.

Dad came around to shake Kenji's hand and make small talk, so Alex backed away with Marley.

"What's that all about?" murmured Marley.

"No idea," he whispered back.

"He likes her."

"What's not to like?"

Marley's elbow caught his ribs. "No, I mean really likes her. But how long has she been widowed?"

"Since I was about two years old. Plenty long enough for someone to win her over if he wanted to."

"Hmm. How long has *he* been widowed?"

Alex shook his head. "I'm not sure. A long time. Maybe ten years." He glanced over again. Nonna was watching Dad and Kenji talk. And look at that. Kenji smiled. Alex hadn't known it was possible.

But Tony was not smiling. He stood stiffly beside Nonna's wheelchair as though guarding her. From Kenji? Or from someone else?

Alex leaned to Marley. "Have you met Nonna's live-in nurse yet?"

"No. Is that her Tony's glaring at?"

Maybe it was. The nurse stood on the other side of Nonna's wheelchair, imposing with a hand possessively on the handle. Interesting. Was that what had Tony's feathers ruffled? But Tony was the most easygoing, good-natured guy Alex knew. Hmm.

"Let me introduce you." He pulled Marley over. "Makenna, I'd like you to meet my girlfriend, Marley Montgomery. Marley, this is Nonna's nurse, Makenna Hamelin."

Marley shot a quick questioning glance at him. Right. He'd forgotten to explain who Makenna was besides a nurse. Too late for the moment, as Marley turned back to her. "Pleased to meet you. And I'm so glad Marietta has someone living with her who can take care of her."

"I go by Johnson, actually. Nice to meet you, Marley. You're the artist, right?"

Marley's face flushed, but she answered cheerfully. "That's me."

Alex's gaze shifted beyond the women to Tony. What *was* his cousin's problem? Surely, he knew he couldn't be there for Nonna twenty-four-seven. No one expected it of him, even the opinionated aunts. He had a brand new restaurant to run. And, even though Alex rarely saw his new tenant, Grayson, it wasn't like he could boot the pilot out because his cousin was disgruntled and looking for new digs.

"Your chickens are charming. Mrs. Santoro purchased two for her bedroom."

"Marietta." Nonna had the tired air of someone who'd made this request a hundred times.

"You did?" Marley let go of Alex's hand as she crouched in front of Nonna.

Alex no longer felt the need to protect his girlfriend

from his nonna. He stepped around them to Tony. "What's going on, man?"

"Nothing, why?" But his cousin's usual cheerful grin was missing.

"You seem on edge."

Tony shot a glare at Makenna. "She'd be enough to curdle anyone's cream."

"Is she mean to Nonna?" Alex's hackles rose at the thought.

"No. She's perfect. Look at her."

Alex looked. Makenna was tall. Blonde. Pretty in a Barbie-doll way with what women liked to call an hourglass figure. He turned back to Tony. "Yeah?"

"She booted me out of my kitchen."

A snort erupted before Alex could stifle it. "Seriously? And I think you mean Nonna's kitchen."

"Oh, sure. You think it's hilarious. Try living with her." Tony's face darkened. "And, of course, I don't mean that literally. I'm sticking to the basement every minute I'm not at the restaurant. She runs a tight ship upstairs, and I'm not welcome, even though she can barely cook."

"For a minute there I thought you were going to tell me she's throwing herself at you or something."

"As if. I'm pretty much married to my career, at least for the next five years. And if I were going to change my mind, trust me, it wouldn't be because of *her*."

That sounded like a lot of protesting. "Well, if you need another kitchen, feel free to come up to the house any day you like. Peter, Grayson, and I wouldn't object to getting some decent meals we don't have to cook ourselves." He couldn't resist a dig. "Though my new tenant makes a mean bacon and eggs. He almost never burns them."

Tony let out a sharp laugh. "Well, that's the sign of a good chef right there."

"It's a decent start for a bachelor pad." Alex chuckled. "Seriously, though, if you need a place to hang out, don't feel you need a further invitation."

"Thanks." His cousin leaned closer, lowering his voice so Alex could barely pick out the words. "Does it weird you out that she used to be your brother-in-law's stepmother?"

"Kind of? But Nathan didn't really know her that way, since he'd been estranged from his dad for years. And Makenna took good care of Maurice while he was dying with little to show for it in the end."

"What kind of woman marries a guy old enough to be her father?"

"That I can't answer. You'd have to ask her."

"Yeah. Not happening. She'll be gone in a couple of months, and Nonna and I can get back to normal."

Alex could only hope his grandmother would recover enough for that. She seemed so small and frail in her wheel-chair compared to the vibrant woman she'd been all his life. He glanced back to Marley, who'd risen to her feet and engaged both Nonna and Makenna in conversation. She was something, his girl.

"You're one of the lucky ones," Tony murmured.

Alex raised his eyebrows at his cousin. "Thought you were married to your work."

"Well, yeah. And a guy can't have it both ways. You take good care of her."

"I will. Trust me. I've learned my lesson."

23

---

*M*arley looked around the community center with its long rows of tables clad in white cloths. Cornucopia baskets spilling half-pint jars lined the centers amid strands of tiny twinkle lights and autumn leaves. She'd helped Sadie, Ava, and Jasmine stir big batches of sugar-free jam for the wedding favors the past few weekends.

"Looks pretty good if I do say so myself." Ava stood beside her, smiling smugly. "To think my big brother finally got married. Nice wedding, huh?"

"It was beautiful." Marley gave Alex's cousin an impromptu squeeze. "But I'm kind of glad it's over." She was ready to have Alex back at her side. He'd spent a lot of time lately fulfilling his best-man duties to Peter, paired with Denae, Sadie's best friend from Montana.

"Not half as relieved as Peter or Sadie, I imagine." Ava nudged her with a wink. "Hasn't Alex popped the question *yet*?"

Marley shook her head. "As though you wouldn't be the first to know."

Ava pumped her fist. "As it should be."

That called for an eyeroll, to say nothing of a change of subject. Today was Peter and Sadie's day, not hers. That was okay. Alex would get around to it when he was ready. "So when are *you* going to find Mr. Right?"

"Do you know how old and married — and did I mention old? Or married? — all the other teachers are? Oh, and mostly female in the elementary schools I substitute in. I was clearly not thinking this career choice through."

Marley linked her arm through Ava's. "At least you *have* a career."

"Tell me again how many paintings you've sold in the past five months."

"That doesn't count."

"Excuse me? It totally counts." Ava's gaze shifted beyond Marley as the door opened. "Finally. The wedding party."

Which meant Alex.

Marley turned and filled her eyes as he stepped into the community center with Denae's hand tucked at his elbow. Both of them were laughing along with Jasmine and Nathan right behind them. Denae wore a pumpkin-toned sheath that matched Alex's shirt.

Alex looked amazing in a black tux, she thought for the hundredth time that day. She'd been unable to keep her gaze off him as he stood beside his cousin at the front of the church. The tux fit him like it had been tailored for him. Maybe it had. But it wasn't just his lean physique. He'd let his hair grow just enough for his curls to show. They were gelled to within an inch of their life. She should know —

she'd touched their crispy tips and couldn't wait to mess them up a little later when this show was over. See those blue eyes up close again, sparkling just for her.

He looked her way now, and their gazes held for a few seconds. His smile softened, filling her with warmth and delight. Then he seemed to remember his duties. He swept a bow to the entire gathering. "Please welcome Peter and Sadie Santoro!"

The newlyweds strolled into the community center, beaming amid shouts, whistles, and camera flashes. Peter pulled Sadie into his arms and kissed her, long and deep, and the crowd's frenzy increased.

"But think of the children!" hollered someone. Alex's cousin Rob, maybe? The Santoro men all sounded a bit alike.

Laughter exploded along with more clapping, and Peter led his bride toward the head table along the far wall. Denae followed, but Alex took a detour to Marley's side. "It's almost over," he whispered, hugging her. "It's been an honor, but I've missed you." He kissed her lightly.

"Me, too." She smiled up at him, straightened his collar, and fingered his boutonniere, where a gerbera daisy and a sprig of purple lisianthus nestled in a bit of greenery. "But first, you need to wow everyone with your oratorical skills."

He grinned. "Duties of a best man nearly fulfilled." He swept her another kiss before turning for the head table.

"Oh, how the mighty have fallen," whispered Ava, tugging Marley toward a nearby table. "I never thought ole cousin Alex would turn into such a softie."

Marley was beyond blushing at Ava's jests. She was just jealous, that was all, but Marley was thankful for her friendship. If Sadie and Peter hadn't opted for a tiny wedding party, Ava wouldn't be free to hang out with Marley at the reception. Since Ava didn't seem to mind, it worked out well for Marley.

"I meant to ask you who those people are." Marley poked her chin toward the other end of their long table, filled with half a dozen families she didn't know, but with Eden and Jacob and their infant twins in the midst of them. "Out of town relatives?"

Ava shook her head. "They're from Green Acres Farm in Idaho. Two of the women are Jacob's sisters. Sadie spent a lot of time up there this past year. One of Jacob's sisters has been mentoring her and coaching her with weight loss."

Sadie was thinner than she'd been when Marley first met her, but needing a coach and mentor for it? "How much did she lose?"

"Over one hundred pounds," whispered Ava. "You wouldn't believe it to see her now."

Marley looked over to the head table where Sadie stood beside Peter. She looked stunning in a white sheath. One hundred pounds? Whoa. "I can't imagine."

"She's amazing." Ava leaned closer, lowering her voice in a conspiratorial whisper. "Hailey and Astrid created a sugar-free wedding cake. I bet none of the guests even notice."

"They've come up with some good recipes for the bistro. I'm willing to give it a taste." Marley let her gaze scan the room. "It's not often I see your grandmother without Makenna these days."

"They gave her the weekend off. She doesn't get many. Tony's parents are staying at the house for Thanksgiving, and Aunt Connie is helping Nonna." Ava looked pensive. "Nonna's recovering okay, but she's definitely not where she was before she fell."

"I still feel so bad—"

"Don't. Oh, look, there's Uncle Ray coming to the microphone. They're finally going to get this show on the road."

The sooner the dinner was over with all the speeches, the sooner Marley could dance with Alex... and begin dreaming of her own future. With him.

∽

IT HAD BEEN A LONG DAY. A long week. With all the guy cousins Peter had, Alex was honored to be the one chosen to stand up at the wedding. They'd become super close being housemates the last couple of years, and the house would seem so empty without his cousin in it. He'd only be next door, of course, but married. Fully focused on his bride, as it should be.

Alex ushered Denae onto the dance floor. It hadn't taken the Santoro men long to get rid of all the tables and most of the chairs after dinner. If a couple of the younger ones had slipped out for a few minutes on a different mission, no one had seemed to notice, but Alex received Evan's thumbs-up with a nod.

At the end of the official wedding party dance, someone tapped his shoulder. Alex turned to see Basil flicking his thumb to get rid of him. All Basil's attention was on Denae. "May I have this dance?"

Trust his older brother to make a move on the visitor, but she seemed well able to handle herself. And this freed him for Marley. Finally.

She and Ava had watched from the sidelines, but as soon as he looked her way, she smiled straight at him. She was stunning tonight in a purple gown, her long hair bound up in a stylish bun. Gorgeous woman. His. *Thank You, Jesus.*

Alex bowed over her hand. "Care to dance?"

"I thought you'd never ask."

Ava snickered and rolled her eyes, but Alex ignored his cousin. One day her time would come, and he'd be the one to tease. Meanwhile, he had a dazzling and precious woman to hold in his arms, one so strong and yet so fragile.

She fit snugly against him as he cradled her close. That bun was going to have to go soon, though. Whatever held it in place stabbed his nose. For now, he'd adjust around it, reveling in her hand on his shoulder, her other hand clasped in his. Her shining eyes meeting his, full of trust and love.

Marley made giving up his uber-structured life worthwhile. He'd been as stuck in his ways as Nonna before Marley moved in next door. He was ready to take the change all the way to the bank. Or the altar.

Peter caught his eye from across the room, raising his eyebrows. Alex nodded then flicked a glance at Evan and Dominic. The two of them saluted and headed for the door.

Still dancing, Alex steered Marley in that direction as well. When the song ended, he whispered, "Want to catch a breath of fresh air? There's so many people in here." Not that half wouldn't follow them.

"Sure."

"Want your coat?"

She looked at him, puzzled. "The cold will feel good, I think."

"Okay." He wasn't going to let her get cold. Not at all. He opened the door and ushered her outside.

Across the street, strings of white lights wound through the fence around the basketball court flashed on.

Will you marry me?

"Oh!" Marley clapped her hand to her mouth. "Someone is proposing...?"

His cue. Alex dropped to one knee and popped open the midnight blue satin box in his hand.

Marley turned to look up at him before realizing he wasn't there. Her eyes widened as she took in his position. As she realized what it meant.

He cleared his throat. "The someone proposing would be me. I love you, Marley. My life changed forever the day I came home to find chickens in my yard. You've kept me off kilter ever since, and I mean that in the very best way. Sweetheart, will you marry me?"

She danced a little jig as she looked from him to the fence then back again. "Alex! Yes!" She bent and kissed him where he knelt.

Alex plucked the ring from its nest and slid it onto her outstretched hand.

In his periphery, the question threaded onto the chain-link fence disappeared, replaced with the word *Yes!* flicking on and off. A wild cheer rose up as the Santoro clan — indeed, the entire neighborhood — flooded out around them.

He'd ignore them all a moment longer. Alex rose and gathered Marley close, covering her mouth with his, every cell in him thrilling with her eager response. Soon. Soon this woman who'd brought vibrant color to his life would be his to cherish forever.

Marley was an adventure waiting to happen.

DEAR READER...

Thanks for reading *Glimpses of Gossamer*! I'm so honored that you chose to spend the last few hours with Marley, Alex, and me. You are appreciated.

I'm an independent author who relies on my readers to help spread the word about stories you enjoy. Would you take a few minutes to let your friends know? Facebook, Twitter, Goodreads... wherever you hang out online.

Also, each honest review at online retailers means a lot to me and helps other readers know if this is a book they might enjoy. I'd sure appreciate your help getting word out.

I welcome contact from readers. At my website, you can contact me via email, read my blog, and find me on social media. You can also sign up for my newsletter to be notified of new releases, contests, special deals, and more! Click here to subscribe. You'll receive *Promise of Peppermint*, the novella that introduces Bridgeview — Rebekah and Wade's story — absolutely free as my thank you gift!

Keep reading for a sneak peek of the next Urban Farm

Fresh Romance book, *Lavished with Lavender* (Makenna and Tony's story). Enjoy!

   - Valerie Comer

   www.valeriecomer.com

   http://valeriecomer.com/subscribe

THE NINTH URBAN FARM FRESH ROMANCE
Lavished with Lavender
USA Today
Bestselling Author
VALERIE
COMER

CHAPTER 1

Lavished with Lavender
An Urban Farm Fresh Romance 9

*S*itting in her car at the curb was not going to get Makenna Johnson this position. She took a deep breath and stared at the white stucco house. Four women waited inside to see if she passed muster as an acceptable caregiver for their mother-in-law's convalescence.

Marietta Santoro. The world's bossiest busybody.

Makenna's late husband's derisive voice echoed in her head. But then, Maurice Hamelin never had anything good to say about anyone, his wife included. She'd stuck with him, though, a man thirty years her senior. If she could handle Maurice, she could handle Marietta.

And she needed this job.

Show time.

She breathed a quick prayer, slid out of her car, and strode up the walk. Before she could reach for the doorbell, the door swung open, and a woman of about sixty offered a bright smile.

"Hi. You must be Makenna? I'm Genevera Santoro. Come on in."

Makenna gave the woman's hand a firm shake. "Yes, that's me. Pleased to meet you."

Genevera introduced her cohorts: Grace, Winnie, and Betta. Together, they made up the local contingent of the old lady's daughters-in-law.

Makenna smiled and nodded at each of them in turn before taking in the living room packed with the evidence of a full life. Furniture, knick knacks, and two walls crammed with ornately framed photos of graduations and weddings and babies.

Maurice had rejected her notion of hanging anything, even an old painting from the thrift store. Certainly not portraits of his sons, since he'd despised them. The feeling had been mutual.

"Please, have a seat." Genevera motioned toward a club chair. "Can I get you a coffee?"

"No, thank you." This wasn't a social call. Makenna perched on the edge of the seat and launched into her spiel. "I achieved my Bachelor of Nursing at Gonzaga U ten years ago and worked at the nursing home for several years before taking time away to nurse my late husband through his final days. Since then, I've picked up shifts at Deaconess Hospital, but nothing permanent full-time, so I applied with the home-care agency."

"Your references are impeccable," Winnie assured her. "And the agency highly recommended you."

They'd better have.

"Tell us a bit about yourself." Grace leaned forward. "What are your hobbies?"

Makenna blinked. Hobbies? Who had time for anything like that? "I prefer to work."

Genevera smiled. "You can't work all the time, though. Do you enjoy reading? Knitting? Gardening?"

Right, the Bridgeview area of Spokane was particularly big on gardening. Makenna had circled the block earlier and caught glimpses of Marietta's lush backyard through the tall fence. She'd probably be expected to help with the old lady's yard. Marietta sure wouldn't be doing much over the next few months, not with a cracked pelvis, broken ribs, and her arm in a cast after a nasty fall a couple of weeks ago.

"Sure, I like gardening." Makenna liked whatever would get her this position. Anything to get away from the head nurse on her ward, who seemed to have it in for her. As if Makenna could help attracting crude remarks from little old men. Maurice had been adept at them, too.

"And you're okay with moving in for a few months? From what the doctor at the rehab center said, Mamma will need assistance through the remainder of the year."

"Yes, I'm fine with that. I can sub-let my apartment."

"It entails more than nursing." Winnie eyed her. "Cooking, cleaning, running the household..."

"No problem." She might not be the most inventive cook, but she could get meals on the table. It would work out. And cleaning? That filled any spare time. She already itched to dust the baseboards and straighten a crooked frame. "Which is your mother-in-law's favorite chair? Will she be able to access it from her wheelchair?"

Winnie pointed to a wide armchair with low arms. "She loves to sit there where she can watch the street. She usually has a knitting project on the go, but I guess she won't be doing that for a while. Not with her arm in a cast."

"You'll need to remove one of the side tables by her chair." Makenna glanced around the living room. "The entire space is too crowded for a wheelchair."

"Yes, the agency did a home study." Genevera nodded. "We have a list of requirements from a ramp to the front door to grab bars in her bathroom to... well, the list is long."

"We have a family work day planned," put in Grace.

"Good. What day do they expect to discharge her?" As in, what would Makenna's start date be?

"Wednesday afternoon, if we're ready. It will be a push for us, but they need the rehab bed for someone else."

"Does that work for you?" asked Winnie. "The agency said they could provide a wheelchair-accessible van to bring her home."

Today was Friday. Makenna nodded. "Wednesday is fine. I can pick her up from the unit and bring her here. I'd prefer to move in the day before if at all possible. At least, if I've met with your approval, and you'd like to hire me?" She held her breath a moment, watching the women glance at each other. *Please, please, please.*

"May I show you around the house?" asked Betta. She'd been rather quiet through the whole interview.

"Sure." That would give the others time to consult behind her back. Whatever. Makenna rose and followed Betta into a large kitchen lined with granite countertops. "This is nice." More than nice. It was a dream kitchen for a serious cook, probably four or five times the size of the one in Makenna's apartment. But then, she normally made do with quick, basic meals.

"Mamma loves to cook." Betta pointed out the doors to

a patio where grapes dangled from the roof supports. Beyond it lay a yard lined with raised beds filled with tomato plants and others Makenna didn't recognize. "And she loves her fresh ingredients. Don't worry, her grandchildren will take care of most of this garden."

Whew. The sound of a gate clicking caught her attention, and a man in denim shorts and a gray T-shirt rounded the corner of the house.

"There's Tony now. Have you met him before?"

Makenna shook her head, but she wasn't sure. All the Santoro guys looked a lot alike with their wiry builds, dark curly hair, and striking blue eyes.

"Tony lives in the basement right now. He's very busy with his new restaurant. You may have noticed Antonio's just a few blocks away?"

Makenna blinked. She'd driven by at times over the winter and watched the transformation of a nondescript building to an inviting Mediterranean-style villa. She should have guessed it was a Santoro enterprise. "Yes, I've seen it."

"Don't worry. My nephew isn't here much. He won't be in your way."

Just the thought of someone else coming and going at odd hours was enough to be in Makenna's way.

Betta opened the patio door and leaned out. "Tony! I'd like you to meet one of the applicants for nursing Nonna."

His head came up, and he met her gaze with assessing eyes. "Hi, there." He came inside the back door. "I'm Tony. And you are...?"

"Makenna Johnson," supplied Betta.

His eyebrows rose. "Johnson? That's not what I heard."

Makenna straightened her shoulders and stared back. "I go by Johnson again." There was no keeping Maurice a secret, not when she'd lived less than a mile from here for six years as his wife. Besides, Grace Santoro, at least, knew who she was. "It's the name on my nursing diploma."

Betta's gaze zipped between them. "Is there a problem, Tony?"

"I don't know. Is there a problem... Ms. Johnson?"

☙ ⸱ ❧

WHAT HAD COME OVER HIM? His words sounded challenging. Mean, even. So not like him.

Tony Santoro had known his aunts were hiring a nurse for Nonna. His cousin Jasmine had told him her late father-in-law's fourth and final wife was on the short list of prospects. She'd even mentioned that Makenna was quite a lot younger than Maurice had been.

He hadn't been prepared for a blond bombshell.

Back when he and his sister had been kids, Gina had been obsessed with her fashion doll collection. This nurse jogged his memory with her long wavy hair, tanned skin, and hourglass figure.

Her chin came up and steely gray eyes bored into his. "There is no problem, Mr. Santoro."

"Tony?" Aunt Betta was all but wringing her hands. "What's going on?"

He hadn't reacted this strongly to anyone in years, negatively or positively. And this was definitely negative. How could someone who looked so... perfect... take good care of his beloved grandmother? How many hours did she spend on those fingernails, anyway?

Tony turned away. "I need to pick the tomatoes before I

head down to the restaurant. We're featuring Caprese tonight."

"Tony?" asked Aunt Betta again.

"He may have known me as Makenna Hamelin." The nurse's words clipped out. "I believe my resume mentions my time as Maurice Hamelin's nurse through his final days." She took a deep breath. "Your sister-in-law Grace knew I was married to him."

Tony couldn't resist one last poke. "What did he die of, Ms. Johnson?"

"Cirrhosis of the liver, Mr. Santoro. He was a heavy drinker, and it caught up to him." She leaned a little closer, her heels putting her eyes on level with his. "If you think I married him for his money or helped him to his death, you accuse me unjustly."

"From what I heard, he had no money."

"Exactly."

"So why did you marry a man old enough to be your father?"

He'd thought her gaze direct and steely before, but it sharpened considerably. "I don't see it as any of your business, Mr. Santoro."

"You're right. Excuse me." He meant from the rudeness of his question as well as from Nonna's breakfast room. Tony reached for the knob on the patio door behind him.

Makenna turned to Aunt Betta. "The information truly didn't seem to be necessary on a professional document. My marital history has no bearing on whether or not I'm a good nurse."

Aunt Grace strode around the table, hooked her hand around Tony's arm, and guided him outside. The door clicked shut behind them.

Tony felt like a little kid who'd been caught misbehaving as he looked down into his aunt's eyes. "I'm sorry. I shouldn't have—"

"We need a nurse for your nonna, Tony."

He braced himself. "I know."

"And, frankly, she's the best of the lot who applied. I knew she'd been Maurice's wife. If anything, I applaud her for staying with him until the end. The man cannot have been easy to live with."

That was a different spin, but it made sense. Tony nodded.

"However, we'll keep looking if there's going to be a problem between you and her. There was another woman closer to my age who applied, but she had back surgery three years ago, and I'm worried she might not be strong enough to assist Nonna. Plus, she doesn't wish to move in."

Nonna wasn't a tiny woman. Sturdy might be the most polite way to put it.

"So we need to know if it's a problem. Because we need the best possible person for your nonna, but you do live here, too."

Tony took a deep breath and let it out slowly. "I'm really not here very much. The restaurant takes up so much of my time."

Aunt Grace nodded. Waited.

He shoved his hands through his hair. "Do what's best for Nonna. It's just for a few months. I'll stay out of Makenna's way."

"What about her struck you negatively?"

It seemed petty to say because of her looks. There was only so much a person could do about the... assets... God had given them. Although it looked to him like Makenna was both aware of her features and knew how to use them to her best advantage.

"She reminds me of someone." A fashion doll, but Aunt Grace didn't need to know that. Besides, would a real airhead have a nursing degree? Unlikely. "It's not her fault. If you truly believe she's the best person for Nonna, go ahead."

Aunt Grace squeezed his arm. "Thank you. I'll let you know what we decide, but we are leaning toward offering her the position. Either way, we'll have a family workday on Wednesday to arrange things for a wheelchair and a hospital-style bed for Nonna. I hope you'll be able to spare a few hours to help out, but if not, we understand."

No doubt all his cousins would take the day off work and show up en force, but could Tony do the same? Nope. Not without closing Antonio's and giving his staff the night off. "I can pitch in for a couple of hours in the morning. Or I can fix lunch for the work crew if that's more help." Nonna's kitchen was a pleasure to cook in.

"Lunch would be great. Thank you." Aunt Grace turned toward the door then glanced back at him. "You won't regret having Makenna around, Tony. It will be a relief for all of us, including you, to have someone caring for Nonna."

He looked through the glass door to see Makenna and the aunts watching him and Aunt Grace. Makenna's perfect eyebrows rose as she stared coolly at him.

Tony stifled a snort. Relief to have her around? Not hardly.

ABOUT VALERIE COMER

Valerie Comer's life on a small farm in western Canada provides the seed for stories of contemporary Christian romance. Like many of her characters, Valerie grows much of her own food and is active in the local foods movement as well as her church. She only hopes her imaginary friends enjoy their happily-ever-afters as much as she does hers, shared with her husband, adult kids, and adorable grand-daughters.

Valerie is a *USA Today* bestselling author and a two-time Word Award winner. She writes engaging characters, strong communities, and deep faith into her green clean romances.

To find out more, visit her website at www.valeriecom-er.com, where you can read her blog, explore her many links, and sign up for her email newsletter, where you will find news, giveaways, deals, book recommendations and more. You can also find Valerie blogging with other authors of Christian contemporary romance at Inspy Romance.